W9-BXS-927

SAN ANTONIO
SUNSET

Other books by Kathleen Fuller:

Special Assignment
Santa Fe Sunrise
San Francisco Serenade

SAN ANTONIO SUNSET

•

Kathleen Fuller

AVALON BOOKS
NEW YORK

Published by Thomas Bouregy & Co., Inc.
160 Madison Avenue, New York, NY 10016

Library of Congress Cataloging-in-Publication Data

Fuller, Kathleen.
San Antonio sunset / Kathleen Fuller.
p. cm.
ISBN 0-8034-9767-9 (hardcover : alk. paper)
1. San Antonio (Tex.)—Fiction. I. Title.

PS3606.O553S23 2006
813'.6—dc22
2005036582

PRINTED IN THE UNITED STATES OF AMERICA
ON ACID-FREE PAPER
BY HADDON CRAFTSMEN, BLOOMSBURG, PENNSYLVANIA

To Erin, editor extraordinaire.

Chapter One

San Antonio, Texas
August, 1850

"**M**a? I'm heading out to the field now. Ma . . . did you hear me?" Jeremiah Jackson stood in the doorway of the modest ranch house and listened for his mother's reply. When he didn't hear her speak, he turned around and walked over to her. She sat in an old wooden rocking chair, staring unseeingly into the snapping, flickering flames in the fireplace. He looked down at her for a moment before kneeling beside her chair. "Ma?"

She didn't turn to him. Not that he'd expected her to. She'd been like this for the past three months, ever since they'd heard that the

Treaty of Guadalupe had been signed with Mexico, ending the war that had taken his brother Luke to California. The conflict had dug its deadly fangs deep into his family. His father and his oldest brother, Thomas, were killed at the Alamo. And as for Luke . . . well they hadn't heard from Luke in a long time. They should have gotten word by now that he was safe by now. That he was coming home. But so far . . . nothing.

With each passing day, Katherine Jackson retreated further inside herself. Although he'd been sympathetic at first, Jeremiah wanted to shake her sometimes to remind her that he was still here. That he would keep taking care of her, just as he had since he was fifteen, when Luke left them three years ago to go to California and fight. Yet somehow those reassurances weren't good enough.

Which meant he wasn't good enough.

With a sigh he rose from the floor. Reaching for his hat on the peg near the door, he slapped it on his head and walked onto the porch. Moving down the steps, he let out three quick whistles. Immediately a shaggy, ragged dog with one eye appeared by his side.

"Good boy, Samson." Jeremiah scratched behind the dog's oversized ears. "Ready to do some work?" A bark accompanied by an enthusiastic tail wag was his reply. Jeremiah rubbed Samson's head, smoothing his short, wiry hair. The dog had shown up on his doorstep two years ago, his skin hanging from his bones, limping from a broken forepaw. It had been touch and go for a while, but Jeremiah had nursed him back to health. Although Samson wouldn't win any beauty prizes, he was an amazing herd dog, and a pretty good hunting dog to boot.

Striding to the barn, Jeremiah tightened the thin strip of rawhide that secured his shoulder length hair at the nape of his neck. It would be a hot one today. After mounting Pepper, the Appaloosa he'd had since childhood, he and Samson went to the sheep pen. He opened the gate, and the sheep spilled out in a bleating mass, eager to graze on the tender grass for their breakfast.

Twenty minutes later, they reached the pasture. Jeremiah dismounted from Pepper, then wiped off the beads of sweat pooling on his forehead. A man could fry an egg on his body in this kind of August Texas heat. He felt as if he was melting from the inside out, and it was still mid-morning. The afternoon would be brutal.

Tipping back his frayed, wide-brimmed hat,

he surveyed the sheep scattered on the plain, their noses to the ground, chomping on sweet blades of grass. Pride swelled within him. In the three years since Luke had left for the war, Jeremiah had expanded the flock from twenty-five stragglers to over two hundred. It was an accomplishment any man would be proud of.

The sudden distant sound of hoof beats caused him to turn from examining the sheep. Samson barked and came alongside Jeremiah as a lone rider approached them. By the huge size of the man seated on the horse he could tell it was Arthur Bannock, one of two ranch hands Jeremiah had to hire when the work had gotten to be too much for him to handle alone. At age forty-eight, Arthur was thirty years older than Jeremiah, but Jeremiah had quickly earned the older man's respect and trust. His brothers and father had always treated him like a little kid, but his employees treated him like the boss.

"Mr. Jackson! Mr. Jackson!"

At Arthur's urgent tone Jeremiah sprinted toward him. "What's wrong? Did something happen to Ma?"

Arthur yanked hard on the horse's reins. "Mr. Jackson, there's someone coming! A small covered wagon coming up the trail."

"Covered wagon?" They rarely had visitors on the ranch, since it was a pretty far piece from the main city of San Antonio. Besides, his mother never had company anymore. "Did you recognize it?"

"No." Worry lines creased Arthur's forehead. "I ain't never seen this one before."

"Stay here with the flock. You too Samson," he added, knowing the dog would follow him anywhere. He ran over to his horse and hurled himself into the saddle, then urged Pepper into a gallop. Ma was home alone.

The wagon was within a few yards of the house by the time Jeremiah had reached the front porch. "Whoa!" he shouted, giving Pepper's reins a hard yank. Jerking his horse to a halt, he jumped off it and ran into the house. "Stay put, Ma," he yelled as he grabbed the rifle hanging on the pegs over the front door.

Her movements slow and stiff, she rose up from her rocking chair near the fire, a vacant look in her light blue eyes. Even though the room was hot as blazes, she pulled her shawl around her thin frame. "Jeremiah?"

"Nothing for you to worry about, Ma," he said, forcing a neutral tone. Glancing back he gave her a reassuring nod, strictly for her benefit. Inside he was working hard to settle his own nerves as he heard the driver shout for his team to stop.

Without another word she resumed her place in the rocking chair and gazed at the fire again.

Gripping the gun, Jeremiah slowly opened the door, hinges squeaking in protest. With deliberate, guarded movements he stepped out onto the porch, clutching his gun at the ready.

The driver was nowhere to be seen. Muffled voices came from the back of the wagon. The canvas cover shook and swayed as if there were people inside. His finger caressed the trigger, but he waited patiently for the occupants to appear. No need to get riled up . . . yet.

"Raul, *cayete!*" a male voice hissed.

Mexicans! Jeremiah whipped up his gun and aimed it straight in front of him. The voice had sounded young, but he wasn't taking any chances. Sure, the peace treaty had been signed, but that meant little to him. Mexicans killed his father and Thomas, and possibly Luke too—he wasn't about to allow them on his land. "Show yourself! *Pronto!*"

A tall figure immediately appeared. A weather-beaten hat perched low on his head, obstructing his features. He walked with a slight limp, and a fine layer of trail dust coated his clothing and boots. Tipping back the brim of his hat, he looked Jeremiah in the eye.

"Luke?" Jeremiah squinted as the man moved toward him. Then a smile broke out on his face as he lowered the gun. "Ma! Ma! Luke's home!"

Jeremiah ran toward his brother, hardly believing that his brother was standing right in front of him. They clasped their arms around each other in a quick, but fierce, hug.

"You're not so little, *little* brother." Luke grinned as he sized Jeremiah up and down. "Heck, you're even taller than me now."

Without thinking Jeremiah straightened, realizing Luke was right. He was taller than Luke, more muscular too, from what he could tell.

"And what's this?" Luke reached around and tugged on Jeremiah's hair. "If it weren't for those green eyes of yours, you could easily pass for an Indian."

Jeremiah studied his older brother for a moment. He looked the same—broad shoulders, brown eyes, always a shadow of beard shading his cheeks and chin. Yet he was different. His features were harder now. His eyes wiser. His stance more guarded, as if he were used to being on constant alert.

But Luke was smiling as he spoke, and there was a familiar teasing tone to his voice. Inexplicably it made Jeremiah feel like a little kid again.

"Luke? Is that really you?"

Both men turned at the sound of Katherine's voice. A lump formed in Jeremiah's throat as he saw his frail mother step off the wooden porch and move toward them. Quickly, he went to her side and offered her his arm. To his surprise, she ignored it.

Luke swallowed. "Ma." In two strides he was standing in front of her. "Yes. It's me."

"Oh, my Lord." Her voice quaked. "The Almighty has heard my prayers. You've come back to me. My boy has come back home." She fell into his arms and sobbed. "My boy has come back home."

Jeremiah looked on as Luke held their mother close, stroking the flyaway strands of her thin gray hair. His questioning gaze met Jeremiah's, concern filling his dark brown eyes. Concern and . . . reproach. Jeremiah frowned.

Suddenly the sharp, squalling sound of a baby's cry pierced the air. Luke cast a look over his shoulder at the wagon, then gently extricated Katherine from his embrace. "Sounds like the baby's awake," he said, moving away from her. "I'll be right back, Ma."

Jeremiah's brows shot up. A baby? Luke had brought home a baby? Jeremiah remembered a young man's voice rebuking someone named Raul moments earlier. Just how many people were in the back of that wagon?

Katherine moved to follow Luke, but Jeremiah touched her arm. "Ma, I think you should stay here."

She faced him, her chin lifted in quiet defiance. "My son is home, and I'm not letting him out of my sight." She turned away and went after Luke, a spring in her step that Jeremiah hadn't seen in a very long time. There was nothing else left for him to do but trail behind.

"I've got her," he heard Luke say as they neared the back of the wagon. "Melanie, honey, I'm sure. Just get the boys out. I'll take care of Rosalita."

When they reached Luke, Jeremiah's eyes widened. He saw something he'd never thought he'd see: his brother holding a baby. A Mexican baby. And that wasn't all. Standing beside him were three dark-haired, olive-skinned boys, the tallest one sporting a beat up American soldier's cap.

In the next second a pretty blonde woman poked her head out of the canvas cloth opening, then hoisted herself down. She tucked a strand of pale blond hair behind her ear, self-consciously smoothing her green dress as she moved to stand by Luke.

"Ma, Jeremiah." Luke cradled the baby in the crook of his arm, wrapping his free arm around the woman's slender shoulders. "This is my wife, Melanie."

She held out her hand to Jeremiah, her mouth curving into a big smile. "It's so nice to meet you," she said, her voice sweet and sincere.

"And these are our children," Luke continued. "Ramon, Rodrigo, Raul . . . and this lively little girl is Rosalita."

Jeremiah didn't speak. He could only stare. Luke's children? His gaze moved to Melanie. With her fair hair and skin, it was obvious the children weren't hers. What was his brother thinking, bringing home Mexican spawn and claiming them for his own?

"Jeremiah," Luke said pointedly.

Melanie was still standing with her hand extended. Quickly Jeremiah grasped it for a split second, then let go. He barely noticed that her smile dimmed considerably.

He turned his attention back to the dusty, dark-skinned children. Had Luke forgotten what happened at the Alamo? How their father and brother and so many other men were slaughtered that day? No quarter, Santa Maria had said. And there had been no quarter. Men and boys, many of them barely older than Jeremiah had been, were killed without mercy by the Mexican Army. Shortly afterward Luke had left Texas, heading west to fight that very same Army. He'd said he'd owed it to their family to continuing protecting what they had died defending—their freedom.

So what in the blazes was he thinking, bringing these children home with him? How could he do this to their mother? He looked at Ma, fully expecting her to be reeling with shock. This had to hurt her. It had to dredge up painful memories, memories that still simmered at the surface for her even on a good day.

Katherine clasped her hands together. "What an adorable little girl!"

Jeremiah did a double take. He watched her reach for the baby, taking her carefully from Luke's grasp. After she murmured a few mushy words in the infant's ear, Rosalita began to calm down. Katherine glanced up and smiled. "She just needed a grandma's touch."

"Yes, she did." Melanie moved next to Katherine, and both women smiled down at the baby, then at each other. Even Jeremiah could tell a bond had been formed.

"We should take her inside," Katherine finally said. "The boys too. I bet they're hungry. Jeremiah, go pick out one of our best lambs for dinner tonight. Hurry, son. Time's a wasting!"

Jeremiah observed Luke and his new family following Katherine into the house. This had to be some kind of cruel trick. Ma talked and chattered as if Luke never had been away, as if she'd known Melanie all her life, and as if the brats were her own blood grandchildren.

And just as it had been when he was a boy, he stood there, separate from his family. Three years of confidence borne out of making a success of the ranch and taking care of what had been left behind simply slipped away. Instantly he was that fifteen-year-old boy again, alone and forgotten. Not the oldest, like Thomas had been. Not the strongest, like Luke always was.

Just Jeremiah. The youngest. The forgotten one.

Chapter Two

"**R**eal good supper, Ma." Luke patted his flat stomach. "Best I've had in a long time." At Melanie's quelling look, he rephrased. "One of the best I've had in a long time."

Katherine laughed. Jeremiah couldn't remember the last time he'd heard such a joyous sound escape her lips. She talked nonstop about how much Luke looked like his father, how beautiful Melanie was, and how charming the children were. She'd said more in the last hour than she had for the past three months.

Jeremiah glanced at everyone eating around the old, scuffed table. Luke was seated at the head, where Jeremiah normally sat. To his brother's right was his wife, and to the left sat his mother. Jeremiah was at the end, surrounded by the noisy, sloppy scamps.

"Have some more potatoes, Ramon," Katherine said, hefting up a huge bowl of fluffy white spuds.

"I'm Rodrigo," the boy corrected as he reached for the bowl. "*Gracias, Señora* Jackson."

Katherine beamed. "Such a polite boy."

Jeremiah scowled. The kids may be polite, but they were nosy, loud, and got in the way. More than once while he was butchering the lamb, he had to tell the youngest boy to get lost, he had been underfoot so much. Now Jeremiah was watching them shovel the food into their mouths, wiping their greasy chins on their sleeves while Melanie and Luke seemed oblivious of them. The only good thing was that the baby had finally stopped squawking, and was asleep in her crib in the corner of the room.

"The ranch is looking good, Jeremiah." Luke wiped the last trace of rich, brown gravy off his plate with a soft slice of bread. "After supper I'd like to take a look at the ledgers."

"Why? You think I haven't kept good records?"

Everyone at the table froze. Katherine gave

him a stern look, but Jeremiah ignored it. "I know where every penny goes," he added.

"I'm sure you do. It's just that I've been gone three years—"

"We all know how long you've been gone. Along with how many letters you sent to Ma. What was it, two?"

"Jeremiah." Luke's voice had an edge to it. "It wasn't like I was off kicking up my heels. I was fighting in a war. There wasn't much time to write letters."

"Of course there wasn't, dear." Katherine took Luke's hand as she looked at Jeremiah. "Jeremiah, show your brother the ledgers after supper. He has a right to see them."

Jeremiah jabbed at a green bean with his fork.

"Gimme," Raul said suddenly.

All eyes turned to the little boy as he snatched the last slice of bread from the oldest boy, Ramon's, hands.

"No!" Ramon took the bread back. "That's mine."

Raul immediately started wailing. "Mine! I'm hungry!"

Melanie immediately got up from the table and went to the young boy. "Raul," she said softly. "You know that's Ramon's. Have some more green beans instead."

"No!" He crossed his arms, his bottom lip jutting out. "I . . . want . . . bread!"

"You should have never taught him to speak English," Ramon said, slowly buttering his piece of bread. With a sly look to Raul, he bit into the soft white slice. "Mmmmm. *Muy bueno.*"

Raul threw back his head and wailed.

"Ramon!" Melanie placed her hands on her hips. "You know better than to tease him. Say you're sorry."

"But he is being a brat—"

"Ramon," Luke warned.

The boy slammed down his bread. "Why do I always have to say I'm sorry? Why can't he say he's sorry for once?"

"Because he's a little boy," Melanie said.

"He is a little brat," Ramon muttered.

Jeremiah's temples throbbed. The walls of the house seemed to close in on him as the ruckus accelerated.

"I want more bread too," Rodrigo chimed in. "And more beans."

"No beans!" Raul shrieked.

With a loud scrape Jeremiah shoved his chair away from the table and shot up from his seat.

He'd had it. Grabbing his hat off the peg near the door, he stormed out of the house.

It was pitch black outside, but he didn't need a light. He could put a blindfold on and still find his way around the ranch. He sensed Samson suddenly appearing at his side. Turning right, they both headed for the stables, which was the only place he would find some peace and quiet.

Striking a match, he applied it to the burnt-tipped wick inside the lantern. The barn flooded with light as he hung the lantern on a metal spike driven into one of the planked wood walls. Samson padded across the dirt floor and flopped down in a small pile of hay in the corner. A low rustling sound came from nearby, and Jeremiah heard Pepper's soft nicker. He snatched up a currycomb and entered her stall, then began running the stiff brush over her sides and withers. When he heard her grunt, he eased up on the ferocity of his movements.

"Is she still a good horse?" Luke appeared in the doorway.

"The best." Jeremiah didn't look up.

The rhythmic chirps of crickets filled the awkward silence growing between the two men. Finally Luke spoke. "I reckon you're wondering about the children."

"Now why would I wonder about that? My brother, who we haven't heard from in over three years, comes home from fighting a *Mexican* war and brings home a passel of *Mexican* children. Oh, and a very un-Mexican wife. What's so curious about that?"

"Listen, Jeremiah, you don't have to be so hardheaded about this."

Jeremiah stilled the currycomb and shot Luke a harsh look. "Oh, so now I'm a hardhead."

"What's gotten into you, boy?"

"In case you haven't noticed," Jeremiah said through gritted teeth, "I'm not a boy anymore."

Scrubbing a hand over his face, Luke took a deep breath. "I know that. Any fool with a decent pair of eyes can see you're a man now. So why don't you start acting like one, instead of a bratty kid?"

Jeremiah turned away, leaning his forehead against Pepper's flank. "I just don't get it, Luke. They're Mexicans." He glanced sideways at Luke. "How could you do this to Ma?"

"Ma seems to be handling it just fine."

"Yeah, she's handling everything just fine, now that you're home."

"What is that supposed to mean?"

Jeremiah threw the comb into the corner of the stall. It hit the wood wall with a hard thud. "Never mind. Look, I'll show you the ledgers in the morning. Then I'll take you to see the sheep, then to meet Arthur and Danny—"

"Arthur and Danny?"

"The two ranch hands I had to hire since you left. There's too much work here for one person to handle."

"Oh, I think I understand now." Luke stepped into Pepper's stall. "You're mad because I left you and Ma alone. I don't know how many ways I can explain it to you, but I had to go. I had to go and fight the Mexicans . . . for Dad and Thomas, for Ma . . . and for you."

"And so you could bring their spawn back."

Luke glowered. "This conversation is going nowhere. Whatever your problem is, don't take it out on my boys. Or my wife. Because I swear, Jeremiah, brother or not, you'll live to regret it." With a soldier's precision, he turned on his heel and left.

Jeremiah balled his fist and hit the side of the stall, startling Pepper. "Sorry, girl." He stretched out his fingers, pain from the punch radiating down the nerves of his hand.

He reached out and touched Pepper's mane for a brief moment, then left and plopped down next to Samson.

Luke had been right. What was wrong with him? Some kind of welcome he'd laid out for his brother. He should go back inside, apologize, and be civil to the children and the wife.

He'd told Luke he wasn't a boy anymore. It was time he stopped acting like one.

Giving Samson one last scratch behind the ear, Jeremiah rose from the hay and headed for the house.

"I just don't get him," Luke said, as he peeled off his shirt. He and Melanie were upstairs in the loft bedroom; the one he, Thomas, and Jeremiah had shared when they were kids. Downstairs in the front room the boys had bunked down for the night. Katherine had taken Rosalita into her room, saying she would get up with the baby if necessary.

Melanie sat at the end of the straw tick bed, brushing her blond hair with long, smooth strokes. "Who? Jeremiah?"

"Yeah." Luke sat down next to her and yanked off his boots. "He acts like he doesn't want me here." Luke paused. "Like he wishes I never came back."

"I'm sure he doesn't feel that way."

"He sure sounds that way. We had a talk out in the barn. It went nowhere. He didn't even want to hear about you and the kids."

"I'm not surprised."

Luke turned to her. "You're not?"

"You didn't exactly welcome the children and me with open arms, if you remember," she gently chided. "It took you a while to get used to us."

He leaned forward and kissed her. "I was an idiot."

"You were human. Just as Jeremiah is. You can't expect him to accept an instant family, especially one as unusual as ours."

"Ma has."

Melanie smiled. "Your mother is grateful you're home. You could have brought home forty children and ten wives and she would have reacted the same way."

"Ugh," Luke said. He scooted back on the bed and lay down, tucking his hands behind his head. "All those children and wives. Now that sounds like work."

She threw the brush at him playfully, then crawled beside him and rested her head on his chest. Immediately his arm wrapped around her shoulders as he turned down the lamp.

"Give him time, Luke. And space."

Luke played with a strand of her silky hair. "How did you get so wise all of a sudden?"

"Our experiences on the trail, taking care of the children, starting our new life together . . . it's changed me the past few months. Sometimes growing up is all it takes to find a little wisdom."

Luke sighed, then tilted up her chin and kissed her. "I reckon Jeremiah has some growing up to do too."

As he approached the porch, Jeremiah saw the lamplight fade from the window in the top part of the house. No doubt Luke and Melanie were up there, sleeping in his loft, leaving him to bunk out on the floor, of course. There went any chance for him getting a good night's sleep tonight.

He opened the front door, but it only moved halfway. He pushed on it again, and it gave the same resistance. Sliding between the partially opened door and the frame, he entered the darkened house and looked down. The door was flush against the backside of a sleeping child.

His hands on his hips, Jeremiah squinted in the dark, barely making out three other shapeless forms lying on the floor. He heard their soft breathing as they slept, taking up almost all the floor space in the tiny front room.

Irritation boiled up inside him. Where was he supposed to sleep? In the barn? Inside the sheep pen? Out in the pasture? He doubted anyone had given his sleeping arrangements a second thought. Just as long as Luke's family was comfortable, that was all that mattered.

Any feelings of goodwill vanished as his frustration took charge of his emotions. Immediately he turned around, accidentally bumping into the kid nearest the door. Instead of waking up, the child merely moaned and shifted in his sleep. Jeremiah wound his way through the front room, grabbing a quilt off the back of his mother's rocking chair and went into the kitchen. He'd bunk in here tonight, but come tomorrow things would have to change.

Three weeks later Jeremiah woke up in his makeshift room in the corner of the barn. The pungent scent of horse manure filled his nostrils, and the hay made him sneeze.

"Jeremiah, you up?"

He groaned at the sound of Luke's voice. His brother sounded like he'd had a good night's sleep. Jeremiah couldn't remember the last time he'd had one. Rising from the cot, he rubbed the back of his sore neck. "Yeah, I'm up."

Luke rounded the corner and walked over to his brother's cot. He loomed over Jeremiah and said, "Ma and Melanie have breakfast ready. After we eat I need you to muck out the sheep pen while Ramon and I take the flock out to graze."

"That's Arthur's job." Jeremiah gave him a belligerent glare.

"Not anymore. I let him go last night."

Jeremiah bolted off the cot. "Let him go? Why did you do that?"

"Didn't need him. We've got Ramon now. He can do Arthur's share."

A hot wave of anger rose inside him. "Then why am I doing Arthur's job?"

"I wanted Ramon to learn how to herd the sheep," Luke explained with irritating calm. He turned and walked out of the barn.

Jeremiah followed him. "Luke, I hired Arthur. Don't you think you should have asked me before letting him go?"

Luke halted his steps and faced him. "I didn't

think it was necessary. It had to be done. We can't really afford him anyway. We have more mouths to feed than before—"

"Because you brought your Mexican brats back here!"

"Jeremiah." Luke's voice dipped low as it always did when he was on the verge of losing his temper. "Watch how you talk about my children."

"I'll speak however I please," Jeremiah shot back. "Wait, you know what, I don't need this. I don't need to be sleeping in a barn, shoveling sheep crap—"

"Jeremiah—"

"You had no right to let Arthur go. Not without consulting me first."

Luke reached out and touched Jeremiah on the shoulder, patting it as if he were eight years old instead of eighteen. "It was for the best, you'll see it in time. Now let's go. We can't keep the family waiting."

"I'm not going anywhere. I'm tired of taking orders from you."

"Now you're just being childish."

"Childish? I guess that's appropriate then, since you've done nothing but treat me like a little kid since you got here. And Ma, she doesn't even know I exist anymore." Jeremiah whirled around and grabbed the leather saddle-bag next to his cot. It held everything he owned—two changes of clothing and fifty dollars. Without another word he pushed past Luke and went to saddle up Pepper.

Luke followed him. "Where are you going?"

"Anywhere but here." He tossed the saddle over Pepper's back and secured it. Grabbing the bridle and reins he fit it on the horse and led it out of the barn. Samson followed at his heels.

"Jeremiah—"

But Jeremiah was finished talking. Hoisting himself on the horse, he slapped the reins and took off. There were better opportunities to be had than living in his brother's shadow for the rest of his life. He could go to San Antonio. Or even out West. Wherever he went, he would earn his own keep, on his own terms. He didn't need them.

He would show Luke. He would show them all.

Chapter Three

Sierra-Nevada Mountains, California
April, 1852

Gold . . . *gold* . . . *gold* . . .

Jeremiah woke with a start, his heart pounding in his thin chest. Inky darkness still cloaked the sky; he had a close-up view of it through the gaping holes in his ratty tent. He moved and heard the bones in his back crack. *I'm too young to feel this old.*

Slowly he sat up. It was before dawn, but he knew he wouldn't go back to sleep now. His dreams had woken him up before. Sometimes he dreamed about striking a good vein of gold, not the little bits of dust he'd been collecting for the past year. Other times, like tonight, he

dreamt that he'd never find what he was looking for. Those were the ones that shook him to
the core.

He glanced at Samson sleeping peacefully
beside him, his head resting on top of his rough
paws. The dog was in sorry shape, almost as
bad as the day he'd arrived at Jackson Ranch.
Months of panning for gold in the mountains
with little success had made both he and Jeremiah scrawny and filthy. But despite his out-
ward appearance, Samson always woke up
happy, his tail wagging, his eyes filled with
hope for another day.

Jeremiah had lost hope a long time ago.

He rolled over and crawled out of the tent, the
ground hard and sharp against his bony knees.
The fire had died out during the night, but he
didn't bother to rekindle it. Instead he sat down
on a rock and listened to the sounds of the
night-crickets chirping, water from a nearby
brook bubbling, a couple of hoots from an owl
way up in a tree. A cold mountain breeze kicked
up, chilling him clear to his bones. He pulled
his threadbare jacket closer to his body, but it
did little to warm him.

How had it come to this? A year ago he'd left
the ranch with high hopes of striking it rich.

The newspaper advertisement he'd found in the barn the night he and Luke exchanged those harsh words had made searching for gold sound lucrative and easy. His plan had been simple enough—he'd stake his claim, find his gold, and return to San Antonio.

He hugged his knees to his chest. Grubby, cold, and starving—this wasn't what he'd envisioned. He'd managed to make something of the Jackson Ranch while Luke was away, but he'd failed to do anything out here in the gold rich mountains.

Sometimes, on quiet nights like this, he would think about Luke. And Ma. Even the rugrats occasionally flitted through his mind. But he could hardly return with his tail between his legs. Not when he'd left the way he did. Not when he was more pathetic than when he came here. He'd arrived in the Sierra Nevada mountains with almost nothing. Now he had less than nothing.

Slowly the sun rose over the jagged crest of the mountain, bathing the air in a soft, pinkish light. Rising from the rock, Jeremiah stretched, his limbs were cold and stiff from sitting for over two hours. He pushed his hair out of his face. It had grown to the middle of his back and

was a tangled, knotted mess. And it would stay
that way, since he couldn't afford to pay someone to cut it in the ramshackle mining town two
miles away.

There was no coffee for breakfast, heck,
there was no breakfast at all. Later he and Samson would scour the area around them for
something edible—berries, maybe a small fish
or two from the stream. But right now, he had
work to do.

Picking up his gold pans, he headed for the
stream that branched from Feather River, and
squatted in front of it. He dipped the pan into
the cold water and shook it, sifting the sand and
silt and extra liquid from the pan, hoping, praying to find something bright and shiny in the
leftover sediment.

All he found was dust.

For the rest of the morning he panned, moving to other locations along the stream. They
were places he knew he'd been to over and over,
yet he was unable to resist searching them
again. He had a feeling deep in the pit of his
stomach that there was gold here, lots of it.

Or maybe he was just hungry. It was dinner-
time after all.

He whistled for Samson, then thrust his pan

in the soft bed of the stream one more time before they went to search for something to eat.
He lifted an extra amount of dirt and rocked the
pan back and forth. As the water cleared, something glimmered from the silt in the bottom.

Jeremiah froze. He squeezed his eyes shut,
then opened them and shook his head. Surely he
was seeing things. But a wave of excitement
flowed through him as he slowly tipped the pan
again, exposing more of the glistening sub-
stance. It wasn't dust. It wasn't the sun playing
tricks on him. And it sure wasn't his imagination.

It was gold, real gold, big chunks of it. Eagerly he picked up one and examined it, turning
it over and over with his grimy fingers. "Samson," he mumbled, his hands shaking. "Samson!" He jumped up, and kept right on jumping.
"We did it. We did it! We finally struck it rich!"

Samson wagged his tail and smiled with his
eyes. It didn't matter that they'd just hit the
jackpot, Samson always wore the same expression anytime he was around Jeremiah. This
time he must have sensed something was different, however, because he barked along with Jeremiah's triumphant cry.

Then Jeremiah stilled. "Shhh," he said, put-
ting his finger to his lips. "Someone might hear

us. You never know when folks might be lurking around, ready to take what's yours." He reached out and patted the dog, then pocketed the gold nugget and returned to panning. He was grinning like a crazed fool. No, he was a crazed fool, but he didn't care. "Dinner will have to wait, boy," he said, eagerly digging the pan deep in the riverbed again. "We've got gold to collect."

Three hours and one hellacious backache later, Jeremiah had mined enough gold nuggets to fill two small leather pouches, ones he had branded with his initials when he first started panning for gold. He tied them to his belt, which was cinched on the last hole but still hung loose on his emaciated frame. He could have found more gold, much more, but for now he had enough to go into Sacramento and live it up a little.

Earlier he had rinsed his body off in the stream, trying to get some of the layers of dirt off his body before heading to the city. He slicked back his hair the best he could. Kneeling before the water, he caught a warped vision of his reflection. His beard was wild, his hair, even though wet, was still unruly. His cheeks were gaunt, his arms thin.

"You've turned into a real mountain man," he said, letting out a low chuckle. Even his pitiful appearance couldn't spoil his mood. Not today. Not when he had enough money on him to buy three barbers if he wanted to. With a grin he stood up and called for Samson. Sacramento wasn't too far—he would be sitting in a steaming hot bathtub in his own hotel room by sundown.

Setting out on foot, he tried not to think about Pepper. He'd had to sell the horse six months ago so he'd have enough supplies to last the winter. Now a man in Down-On-Your-Luck, the mining camp nearby, was using her to help mine further on down Feather River. A tightness grabbed hold of his chest, but he pushed it away. The time for regrets was over. He touched one of the pouches of gold. He held a much brighter future in the palm of his hand.

Jeremiah had walked a couple of miles when Samson veered off into the bushes, his nose to the ground. "Now's not the time to sniff out a rabbit," he said, eager to get to his destination. "Besides, you'll be feasting on steak tonight."

Suddenly he heard the sound of a twig snapping behind him. Halting, his head jerked around as he surveyed the shrubbery nearby. Every sound was magnified in his mind: every whisper of the breeze, every bird singing, every frog croaking. A cold sweat broke out on his palms.

He wasn't alone.

Just as that realization had entered his consciousness, he was slammed to the ground, his cheek hitting a large stone. His breath whooshed out of him. Something came down hard on his lower back, making stars explode in front of his eyes. Instantly he was flipped over. A man's heel pressed on his throat. A gun touched his temple.

"Well, looky what we got here." A man dressed in dusty black forced the round end of the barrel against Jeremiah's head. A dark cloth covered his nose and mouth. "Bart! Get over here."

Black spots danced across the man's face as Jeremiah felt his life squeezed out of him. All sounds seemed faraway, as if he were in a tunnel. Somebody moving. Something scraping against the ground. He barely felt hands on his body, searching him. When he realized they were reaching for his gold he tried to fight back, but he was too weak. The man pressed on his throat even harder.

"Wow, boss, look at all this gold."

Jeremiah's gaze flicked to a hunched over man and the two bags in his hand. His cry of protest lay trapped in his bruised throat.

The man in black grabbed one of the bags, and weighed it in his palm. "This greenhorn sure made it easy for us, carrying his gold for all the world to see. Next time," he said, looking directly at Jeremiah with his hard black eyes, "Ya ought to put these in your pocket. Not that there's gonna be a next time."

Jeremiah heard something rustle in the nearby bush. *Oh no, not now, Samson. Run, hide. Get far away from here.* He looked to the side and saw his dog appear, his scrawny tail wagging happily.

"Get outta here you mangy mutt." Bart kicked Samson hard in the side, sending his thin body careening into the bush.

The dog's whimpers reached Jeremiah's ears, making his blood boil. He tried to move, but the masked man held him firmly in place.

Then Samson's whimpering suddenly stopped. Nothing moved in the bush. Jeremiah weakly clenched his fists, but his anger couldn't be unleashed. He was still firmly pinned to the ground.

The man turned to Bart, hefting the gold. "This should last us a good long while." His voice was slightly muffled behind his bandanna, but his stutter was clear. "The claim shouldn't be too far from here. I bet there's a lot more gold where this came from."

Jeremiah's eyes widened.

The man cackled and looked directly at him. "I reckon I'm right."

"So, ya gonna kill him now?" Bart moved forward, one foot dragging behind him.

Jeremiah squeezed his eyes shut as the masked man slowly cocked the trigger. To his surprise he felt the gun pulling away from his temple.

"There's no sport in killing a man who's half dead," he said, his foot still on Jeremiah's throat. "I'll leave him to ya, Bart. Do what ya want with him."

Bart's eyes gleamed. "Really? Oh, thanky boss. Thanky, thanky."

The man stepped away from Jeremiah, who took a big gulp of air into his starving lungs. "But whatever ya do," he said in a low, menacing tone, "Make sure this sack of horse dung don't follow us." His eyes narrowed. "Make sure he *can't* follow us."

Bart hunkered by Jeremiah and grabbed him by the shirt collar. "Oh, he won't follow us, boss. I promise ya that. By the time I'm done with this scrawny boy, he'll wish he ain't never been born."

Chapter Four

"Calliope. Calliope! Gal, wake up!"

Callie's eyelids fluttered open, still thick with sleep. She was tired, so very tired. All she wanted to do was slip away into dreamland again, where she didn't have to worry about money, or food, or the next foolhardy thing Eli would do. Her lids fell closed again, only to pop open when she heard a sharp pounding sound in her ears.

"Gal, when I say wake up, I mean it!"

She sat straight up, bumping her head on a copper pot hanging from the roof of their tinker cart. Eli was already climbing in the back. The scent of cheap whiskey surrounded him, thick and overpowering. He held a small

39

lantern, flooding the cluttered space with light. She could make out his cloudy eyes, his unsteady movements, his thinning gray hair sticking out in tufts right above his ears. He was drunk—again.

"Eli, you promised you'd stop drinking," she said, rubbing the top of her head.

"I jest has a little sip," he replied, holding his index and forefinger parallel to each other, denoting a tiny amount. "Well, maybe a couple little sips."

"Eli!"

He threw his bedroll at her. "Get dressed, we gotta go."

A sinking lump formed in the pit of her stomach. "Not again. What have you done this time?"

"It ain't my fault, I swear."

She yanked off her blanket. "It's never your fault."

He glared at her. "I was just havin' an innocent game of cards with a couple fellas in town. I was beatin' the pants off 'em too."

Callie groaned. She'd heard all this before, many times, in many towns and in many cities. She had hoped Down-On-Your-Luck would be different for them. She had already gotten a job as a washerwoman for the miners in town—a job she was supposed to start tomorrow. But nothing was different. Once more they were on the run. They were always on the run.

"Had a perfect inside straight draw," Eli continued. Although he was well into his cups, he sounded stone sober. *From years of practice,* Callie thought bitterly. "Then he 'cused me of usin' a marked deck."

"Did you?"

"Heck no." He started rummaging through his clothing trunk. "I learned my lesson back in Nevadey. Ah ha!" Triumphantly he pulled out a pair of worn trousers.

It was at that moment Callie realized he wasn't wearing anything but his long johns. "What on Earth happened to your pants?"

"I'm gettin' to that part." He sat down in the cramped cart and thrust his leg inside the pants. Being a short man had its advantages. "Seems after they realized the deck was clean, they thought I was sneakin' in cards."

Callie got up on her knees and grabbed the brown dress neatly folded beside her makeshift bed. "Surely you didn't do that."

"Well. . . ." He lifted up his backside and jerked up the pants over his red long johns. It took him two tries to accomplish it.

"Eli! You just said you'd learned your lesson."

"About playin' with a marked deck. Passin' off cards is somethin' I ain't tried before."

Callie rolled her eyes. "Let me guess. They chased you, stripped you, found the cards, and you ran." If there was one thing Eli could do, it was run. He was as fast as a jackrabbit, despite his short stature.

"Yep, that's pretty much it. Strange set of fellas, let me tell you. But afore they caught me I won this from 'em." He dug into the protruding breast pocket of his shirt and pulled out two leather pouches nearly filled to bursting. "Gold nuggets, gal. Lots of 'em. Let me tell you they was madder than a wet hen on a cold day that I skinned this offa 'em."

"Eli—"

"Good thing I lost 'em a few miles back; 'parently they ain't from 'round here. But I reckon they'll find me soon enough. They got horses, ya know." He opened the door and exited the cart. "Get a move on, gal! Time's a wastin'!" The door slammed shut behind him.

With a sigh Callie pulled her dress over her long-sleeved nightgown, wincing as she raised her arms above her head. Even though so many years had passed since the accident, the pain was still present in her shoulders and upper back—pain she would have to deal with for the rest of her life.

They'd been staying in Down-On-Your-Luck for only two days, after Eli lost his job at a livery in Sacramento. It was supposed to be much longer than that. Eli had promised that this time they would settle down. He would sober up and find a steady job and a house for them to live in, instead of an old tinker's cart.

For years she had dreamt about living in an actual house. A real home, some place she'd never had to leave again. Although they weren't related, Eli had been taking care of her since she was a young girl. Or at least he had tried to. But as usual, Eli had broken his promise.

He always broke his promises.

She jammed on her shoes and climbed out. The night air was cool, as it always was in the mountains. She was grateful that at least this time Eli wasn't panning for gold. He had done that before in '49, with little success, even after living on a claim for over nine months. She never wanted to see another flat tin pan for the rest of her life.

They quickly gathered the rest of their belongings and loaded them up, attached the lantern to the top corner of the cart, then clambered into the driver's seat. Eli reached for the reins, but Callie snatched them away. "You're drunk."

"That ain't never stopped me afore." He crossed his short, brawny arms like a petulant child.

Hurriedly they traveled away from the town. She didn't bother to ask Eli where they were going. He didn't know. He never did. "We'll end up where we end up," was his standard response.

Lord, she was so sick of living this way.

Within minutes she could hear Eli's loud, grinding snores. She glanced at him. His chin touched his chest, his head swaying and dipping with the jostling movement of the cart.

"At least one of us is at peace," she said into the night.

Suddenly the mules came to an abrupt halt. "Hey!" She grabbed the reins tightly as Eli pitched forward. Callie grabbed the back of his shirt before he was thrown off the cart.

"What the—is we there yet?" he mumbled, shaking his head.

She released him. "Something's wrong with the team." Grabbing the lantern, she hiked up her skirt and jumped to the ground, then made her way to the front of the mules.

"What's the matter? she cooed, touching Gold's back flank. She and Silver, the other mule, remained perfectly still.

When she looked on the ground in front of them, she understood why.

"Oh my God!" She dropped to her knees. "Eli!" She put the lantern beside her, her hand covering her open mouth.

"We ain't got time for this, Calliope." He came up behind her, paused, and let out a low whistle. "Is he dead?"

"I-I don't know." She couldn't bring herself to touch the battered and broken form lying in front of her. He was nearly naked, wearing only the bottom half of a pair of filthy long underwear. His torso was covered with bruises and marks. He was so thin she could count his ribs. One arm was stretched out while the other one was twisted into an unnatural shape. She picked up the lantern and moved it closer to his face. It was a swollen, bloody mess.

"He's dead alright," Eli said matter-of-factly. "C'mon. Let's go."

His callousness horrified her. "We can't just

leave him here. Besides, the mules won't move—"

"They'll go 'round him." Eli cast a quick look over his shoulder. "Calliope, we have to get movin'," he said impatiently. "Right now. No tellin' how close on our tails those card sharps are."

"Hush." Callie raised her hand up to Eli. "I think I heard something."

"You didn't hear nothin', gal. It's your 'magination playin' tricks on you."

Ignoring Eli, Callie bent forward, leaning her ear close to the man's mouth. He moaned.

She popped back up. "He's alive."

"No, he ain't." Eli's tone was cold and stern. He grabbed her arm. "We're leavin'. Now!"

Callie turned around and faced Eli down, yanking herself from his grip. "This man is alive. And we're taking him with us."

"Calliope," Eli warned.

"Eli, take a good look at him. He's skin and bones, he's bleeding everywhere, and I'm sure his arm is broken. We cannot in good conscience leave this man to die."

"And jest exactly how are we gonna take care of him? Huh? You ain't no doctor. Besides, we ain't got the room."

"We'll make room." She turned and looked at the man again. His chest barely moved up and down. But it moved. He was clearly alive. And Callie would do everything she could to save him. "Help me get him up."

Eli hesitated. Then after muttering a few choice words, he bent over and grasped the man's arm. Both he and Callie ducked their heads beneath his shoulders and lifted him. She heard him moan louder.

"Sorry," she whispered as they dragged him to the cart. "We don't mean to hurt you."

"I don't think we could hurt him any worse than he is," Eli said, a little breathless. Although the injured man was thin, he was about two heads taller than Callie, and almost three taller than Eli.

Then something whimpered.

They both stopped and looked over their shoulders. Out of the shadows an animal crawled forward. Gaunt, with knotted fur and protruding ribs, it had only one eye and looked to be in the same pitiful shape as the man.

It looked directly at Callie, and she realized the creature was a dog. It whined again, and somehow she knew this animal belonged to the man. "We have to take the dog too," she informed Eli.

"Heck no! Calliope, I'm puttin' my foot down. Bad 'nuff we have to drag the half-dead with us, but now you wanna take his fleabag? No way, no how."

"Look at him, Eli. He's starving. And he wants his master."

"Ain't seen a more pathetic excuse for an animal in my life. He's missin' an eye, for cripes sake. Bet he's covered in bugs too. Leave him be, gal."

Callie stood her ground. "We're not leaving unless the dog comes with us." She planted her feet firmly in the dirt and refused to budge.

"Calliope—"

"I mean it, Eli!"

"Fine," he said with a grunt. "Have it your way. But they're both yer responsibility, Calliope Walters. I ain't feedin' nor tendin' nor takin' care of either one of 'em. Those strays are yers alone."

Relief ran through her. "Thank you."

Lopsidedly they carried the battered man back to the cart and pulled him inside. The dog jumped in right after him.

"For goodness' sake, Eli, he's a man, not a side of beef. Be careful."

"Calliope, I swear I'm 'bout ready to—" his

voice trailed off and he gave the man one last shove. Callie, who was pulling him toward her, fell back, clonking her head on the cart's wooden wall. "Ow."

"Serves ya right," Eli muttered. "At least I get to drive now."

"No, you don't. You're drunk, remember? You fell asleep two minutes after getting into the buckseat."

"Calliope, we can't stay here. We'll all be dead if we do. I promise I'll stay awake. You ain't got nothin' to worry 'bout."

She didn't believe him, but she also had no choice. Finally she relented. "Just shut the door."

Soon afterward they started moving again. The air in the cart immediately grew thick with the sour aroma of sweat, dirt, dog, and blood, causing her stomach to twist. Steeling her nerves and her constitution, she gently laid the stranger against the rolled up blanket that served as her pillow. Then she grabbed a small lamp and lit it. "Much better," she said. It didn't help the smell, but at least she could see what she was doing.

Looking down at him, she bit her bottom lip. His eyes were swollen shut, and he hadn't uttered a sound since they'd shoved him in the cart. She assumed he was out cold. She couldn't imagine the pain he'd endured from such a beating. Pain was something she understood, something she'd dealt with nearly all her life. Yet what she dealt with on a daily basis didn't compare to what this man had been subjected to.

She didn't know where she should start first. His brutalized face? His slashed up torso? His mangled arm?

"His arm," she decided. It was closest to her. She reached out and touched his elbow.

"Dislocated." She'd seen a dislocated bone before, once a few years ago when Eli had fallen off a ladder while picking walnuts after drinking a full bottle of gin. He'd knocked his shoulder out, and between the two of them and another bottle of liquor, they'd managed to get it back in place.

But she couldn't give this man alcohol to ease his pain. She could only pray he remained unconscious while she set his arm.

Taking a deep breath of fetid air, she rolled up her sleeves and grasped his arm firmly. He flinched. Pity pooled inside her. If that slight contact affected him, there was no telling how he would react to her manipulating his elbow. But it had to be done.

"Ready," she whispered, her heart racing. "Set . . ." With one sharp move she pushed the elbow back in place.

His howl of pain echoed in her ears. The noise was deafening once the dog howled along with him.

"Good gravy, Calliope." Eli's irritated voice sounded stifled through the wooden wall of the cart. "What ya doin' in there? If ya wanted him dead we should have left him behind."

The man's body stiffened, then went limp again. His eyelids moved, but barely. They were too swollen to completely open. He also tried to speak, but his lips couldn't form the words.

"Shhh," she said softly, brushing damp strands of his long black hair away from his face. "That was the worst part." With swift movements she stabilized his arm, using one of her old dresses. She didn't think the man would appreciate wearing a blue and pink calico sling, but it was all she had.

He slipped back into unconsciousness. Callie used her drinking water to wash the blood from his wounded skin. She used whiskey to clean his cuts. Eli really wouldn't appreciate that. She ripped one of her old muslin nightgowns and made bandages. All the while she talked to him, Whispering words of encouragement. She assured him everything would be alright.

She had no idea if he would live to see morning.

The dog had already settled at the man's feet. Exhausted, she slid between his owner and the wall of the cart and lay on her side, curling her body close to his. The position made her back ache even more, but it was all the room she had. This close to him she could see the tangles in his hair and beard. He was a filthy, broken man.

Dear God, she prayed as her eyelids closed. *Please let him last through the night.*

Chapter Five

Jeremiah was in agony.

He tried to move, but he couldn't. He attempted to open his eyes, but they remained shut. Even as he lay motionless, the pain washed over him in alternating sharp and dull waves. Every nerve was on fire, and every inch of him throbbed, his arm especially. He didn't know where he was, only that he must be moving somewhere, as his body rebelled at every bump and lurch. When he tried to swallow, a low moan escaped his throat.

He sensed movement next to him, heard a quiet rustling sound. Felt the cool touch of a soft hand on his forehead. It immediately dulled some of the pain.

"I must have been dreaming," a sweet, melodious voice lilted to his ear. "I thought you were awake."

I am awake. But even as he thought the words he slid further and further into a dark abyss. Still he could hear her talking.

"Everything's going to be alright. I'm not going to let anything happen to you. How could anyone hurt you like this? How can people be so monstrous?"

On and on she talked, her words soothing, her touch healing. He thought she was an angel, and he floated on the current of her voice . . . until he could no longer hear her at all.

The cart lurched to a halt, waking Callie out of a fitful sleep. Above her, copper pots and tin vessels clanged together. Quickly she reached to silence them with her hands, glancing down at the man as she did. She shouldn't have bothered. He didn't make a sound.

She placed her palm above his nose and mouth, keeping it there for a few moments until she was satisfied he was still breathing. She stretched her arms, and tried to straighten her back as much as possible. Her gaze went to the dog, who was sitting up and scratching the back of his ear with his left paw. After checking on her patient one more time, she opened the back door of the cart and stepped down, the dog jumping out after her. The bright morning sunlight streamed into her eyes, causing her to squint.

Briefly she surveyed her surroundings. They were somewhere in the mountains, on a flat, but small patch of land. The dog took off into a nearby thicket, his nose sniffing the dusty ground.

Why would Eli bring them here, instead of going to another town? Then she realized why—it was secluded, the perfect place for hiding from people who wanted to hurt you. Or wanted to see you dead.

"So, has he gone to Glory yet?"

Startled, she jumped at the sound of Eli's voice, and whirled around. "No, he hasn't, and what an awful thing to ask. I can't believe you care so little for a fellow human being."

Eli hitched up his trousers. "Callie, for all we know he could be wanted by the law. You could be playin' nursemaid to a killer or somethin'."

"I seriously doubt that."

"How do you know?"

She paused. He had a point. She had no idea

who the man was, or where he came from. There was one thing she would stake her life on, though. She knew he wasn't a criminal. "I just have a . . . feeling. That's all."

"A feelin'?" Eli shook his head. "You women, yer all about feelin's and emotions and fluffy stuff. I bet you'll be feelin' somethin' when he gets well enough to point a gun at one of us or rob us blind."

"I am not going to argue with you about this." Callie paused. "Where are we?"

"Don't rightly know. Don't rightly care either, jest as long as we stay outta sight for a while."

She waved toward the cart. "But he needs to see a doctor! I can't take care of him here."

"You're gonna have to, gal."

"I'm not a girl!" She crossed her arms over her chest.

"Coulda fooled me." His bright blue eyes were red rimmed, but less cloudy than the night before. He also looked as tired as she felt. "We're not movin' from this spot, Calliope. Not for at least a couple of days. There's water nearby, and I can hunt for game in the mountains. As fer him," he nodded toward the cart. "It's in God's hands whether he'll be makin' it or not. Now unhitch the team. I gotta get me some shut-eye." Turning on his heel, he walked over to a nearby tree and sat down at the foot of it. He crossed one short leg over the other and fell asleep.

Callie fisted her hands. She was exhausted too, and her back ached miserably. Not only did she have to unhitch the team and lead them to grass, but she had to fetch fresh water to refill her drinking jug. Then she had to prepare something for her and Eli to eat, along with some broth for the injured man when he woke up. *If* he woke up.

Wearily she walked over to Gold and Silver and began detaching them from the cart. There was nothing left to do but tend to her chores. Eli wasn't about to help out, she knew that. They had to have water and food, or none of them would be of any use at all.

Leading the mules to the nearby grass, she did what she had to do. She set to work.

Jeremiah awakened, this time forcing his eyes open. His vision blurred for a moment, then cleared. He couldn't see much through the tiny slits of his eyelids, but he could make out a few things. The light was dim, thin slivers of it streaming through the gaps in the wooden slats of the walls of wherever he was lying. Several shiny objects hung suspended above him, and there was a blanket covering his body up to his neck. He was in some type of small, confining space.

But where was the angel? He must have dreamt about being in heaven, because this certainly wasn't it. A smelly cramped place where it looked like heavy pots would come crashing down on him any second while he was powerless to move. It seemed more like hell to him.

Then suddenly everything came back to him. The gold. The man in the black mask. His hunched over henchman. A foot on his throat. A gun to his head. A fist in his face. Then . . . nothing but black.

He remembered Samson, so cruelly kicked into the bushes as if he were a clod of dirt. Jeremiah feebly called out his name. No answer. He hadn't expected one.

He tried to sit up but he couldn't. Every movement felt like a thousand knives plunging into him. He groaned in pain—a pain that not only ravaged his body, but his heart and soul too. Where had they taken him? Why hadn't they just killed him? They'd stripped everything else from him—his gold, his dog, his claim. He lifted his head again, only to fall back with a muffled moan.

Moment's later a blinding light hit his eyes, making them water. All he could see was the light; then a shadow passed over it, then it disappeared completely.

"You're awake!'

There it was, that angelic voice, filled with surprise this time. He moved his lips to speak, but could only utter a raspy sound.

"Don't talk," she said.

He heard the strike of a match, smelled the smoky odor of sulfur. The area brightened. There was barely room for two of them in the space. She scooted alongside his body, leaning over him.

"This is a good thing," she said. "A very good thing."

Even through his slitted eyes he could make out her smile.

"I imagine you're thirsty. I know I would be if I were in your shoes. Wait here and I'll fetch some water." Then she stopped. "Of course you'll wait here. Where else can you go? That was a silly thing to say." She disappeared, and he heard the squeak of a door hinge.

Moments later she returned with a jug. The bubbling sound of water being poured reached his ears. He felt her place her hand behind his head and gently lift it up.

"Easy," she whispered, her face close to his. "Just a tiny sip."

At that moment he realized how thirsty he really was. His mouth was against the rim of the cup but his swollen lips wouldn't cooperate. More fluid dribbled down his chin than went inside him.

"Very good." She sounded as if she were speaking to a two year old—which was fitting, since he felt as helpless as one.

"Wh-where . . . am . . ." he managed.

"Relax." She put her hand lightly on his arm. As before, her touch seemed to lessen his pain. "We'll talk later. Right now you need some sleep. And I imagine some relief." Again she lifted his head and brought the cup to his lips.

"I put some laudanum in the water," she explained. "I hope you don't mind. It will help with your pain. I take it sometimes. It really does work."

Did he mind? Was she crazy? He welcomed anything that would take away the agony. It wasn't long before he was feeling the effects. A heaviness fell over his mind and body.

"There. That's it. Just sleep."

Her voice was soothing . . . faraway . . . silent.

Callie leaned back against the wall of the cart. She expelled a long breath. *Thank God.* It was all she could think of. The man was far from recovered, but at least he woke up. That was a good sign. It had to be.

Fatigue seeped deep into her bones. She had taken care of the team and hauled water from the creek nearby. Eli was still snoring loudly over at the base of the tree. Surprisingly, the dog had joined him, plopping down right beside Eli's sleeping form.

Callie lay down next to the man and closed her eyes. *Just a few winks. A couple of minutes, that's all.* It was the last thought she had before drifting to sleep.

Clark Blanchet kneeled on the ground and dragged his index finger through the cart wheel groove indented in the dirt. It was narrower than a standard wagon wheel. He scanned the area, sensing something familiar about it. He chewed on his cheroot for a minute, then took the lit end of it and stubbed it out in his hand.

"Ouch, boss. Don't that hurt?"

Clark slowly turned around and looked at Bart. "Yep."

"Then why'd ya do it?"

Turning away from Bart, Clark ignored the question. He had to keep a level head. The best way to do that was to transfer his thoughts somewhere else; like to the searing pain in the palm of his hand.

"So what are we gonna do now, boss? We done lost our money."

"Quiet, Bart."

"Who'da thunk it, some little old guy beatin' you at your best game."

"Shut up, Bart."

"And now we got no money, and neither one of us can find that claim. Ya know, the one that belonged to the guy we robbed yesterday? You said it had to be nearby, but I guess it ain't because we ain't seen it nowhere. And how do you suppose we gonna pay back Diamond Joe now? He's gonna want the money you stole from him. I bet he's already in Sacramento right now lookin' for us."

"I said shut up!" Clark whirled around, and

with a flick of his wrist, drew his gun. "Under-stand?"

Bart nodded mutely.

"That's better." Clark holstered his gun and took a moment to weigh his options. His plans had certainly blown up lately. It had all seemed perfect in the beginning. He'd helped Diamond Joe rob the bank in their hometown of San Francisco. Then when the idiot was busy booz-ing it up in the local saloon, he'd grabbed the money, Diamond Joe's horses, and fled. Unfor-tunately, he had picked up an unexpected guest along the way.

Bart had been sitting on top of the horse teth-ered to Diamond Joe's, waiting for his boss to come out of the saloon. When Clark had taken the horse, he had dragged Bart and the other ani-mal with him. The simpleminded man had no loyalty to anyone; he was just as eager to do Clark's bidding as he had been Joe's. Clark had no choice but to stick with him. He couldn't af-ford to have Bart seek out Joe and report on Clark's whereabouts.

But Bart had proved to be more of a liability than he'd bargained for. Two days after the rob-bery, they had been robbed themselves on their way to Sacramento. Now they only had half of what they'd started off with. The gold nuggets would have covered that loss and more, if they hadn't been swindled by that good for nothing piece of trash in Down-On-Your-Luck.

"I think I've been here before," Bart said. Immediately he clapped his hand over his mouth, remembering he had been ordered not to speak.

"Ya have?"

Bart nodded, his palm still pressed against the lower part of his face. "This is where we robbed that guy," he said in a smothered voice. "Don't you remember?"

"Of course I do!" Clark snapped. He wasn't about to admit he had no sense of direction. Sometimes he could follow a map, but when it came to using the land to orient himself he was completely lost. "What did ya do with that greenhorn?"

Bart's eyes widened as his head bobbed back and forth, looking around the area. "I don't know, boss. He was pert near dead when I left him. I beat him up real good. Maybe the coyotes got him?"

"Maybe." Clark looked down at the ground. There were some spatters of crimson in the dusty dirt, but no evidence that a man had been torn apart and carried away to feed some hungry cubs.

Bart suddenly gasped. "You don't think someone took him, do you?"

Clark looked at the cart tracks. "For your sake they better not."

Bart limped over to Clark and stood next to him. "You thinkin' these tracks belong to that little guy?"

"Yes. Looks like they went deeper into the mountains."

"Is that a good thing, boss?"

Clark didn't think so. Everything was already starting to look the same to him; he imagined it wouldn't be any different the further they traveled into the Sierra Nevadas. But he'd get back his gold. He hadn't gone to all the trouble of stealing it only to have it swiped a few hours later by that midget.

He and Bart were on the run anyway, which was why they'd headed to that old mining camp in the first place. Keep a low profile, that was the name of the game.

Until he'd been made a fool of. That he wouldn't tolerate.

"Get the horses, Bart," he said, tossing his used up cheroot on the ground. "It's time to get back our gold."

Chapter Six

"We can't stay in the mountains." Callie stirred the pot of stew hanging over the fire.

"Why not?" Eli lifted his axe and slammed it into a short log, splitting it neatly in two. He tossed the pieces to the side and picked up another one. "We got everythin' we need here, gal. Plenty of water, firewood, fresh game. That puny mutt is a pretty good huntin' dog. Never woulda thunk it."

"Eli, we need more things than that—medicine, for one."

"We'll make due with what we got. For the time bein' at least." He brought the axe down again on the top of the wood. "Until the coast is clear."

"And how will you know?"

He stopped, the axe held midair. "Just like you women have your feelin's, I got mine. And my feelin's telling me those men are still after us." The axe came down again.

Callie shivered and sat down on a small wooden stool. It was close to sundown, and the air had cooled considerably. As they had all day, her thoughts drifted to the man inside the tinker's cart. The laudanum had done the trick—he hadn't wakened since she'd given it to him. But other problems were beginning to surface: how would she take care of his needs? Soon, God willing, he'd be awake much longer, and he'd have to eat and drink and use the privy. He desperately needed a bath. She couldn't count on Eli to help with that.

Somehow she'd have to find some clothing for him, all he had was his long underwear. Eli's castoffs would do for now, but they were almost threadbare; he wouldn't be able to wear them for long.

"Yep, as soon as the coast's clear, we gonna be livin' it up."

Eli's words brought her out of her thoughts. "Living it up?"

"Good food, new clothes . . . and a hot bath for you, gal."

"You might think about a hot bath for yourself," Callie said, wrinkling her nose.

"Nah," he said, tossing aside two more pieces of wood. "I do fine rinsin' off in the creek. Anyways, it's off to Coloradey we go."

"Colorado?"

"Denver. I hear tell it's a nice town, and gettin' richer by the minute now that they done found gold too. They got a fancy hotel—and I reckon a real nice saloon too."

Callie shot up from her seat. "And how are we going to pay for a fancy hotel and a bath and such? We have an extra person to care for—and a dog, don't forget."

"Thanks to you, gal."

"He's going to need medicine and clothes and . . ." She brought her fingertips to her temples, trying to ease the sharp pain that suddenly appeared there. She'd have to carve a dozen or more figurines before she would have enough money to pay for all those expenses.

"Gal, we ain't gonna have to worry 'bout money for a long time."

Her gaze flew to him.

He extracted the pouches from his pocket. "There's 'nuff in here to last us a few years. And 'tween your carvin's and my enterprisin' we'll be sittin' in clover for a good long while."

She arched a dubious brow. "Your enterprising?"

"I got me some idees." He pocketed the pouches and started gathering up the wood in his short stocky arms. "Investin', Calliope. That's what I'm talkin' about."

"You have no idea what you're talking about," she snapped, grabbing her wooden spoon and giving the stew another stir. Every fiber of her being ached, but tonight she wouldn't take anything for the pain. She had to save it for the stranger. He needed it more than she did.

But even though she tried to keep them away, tears came to her eyes unbidden. "I know exactly what's going to happen," she continued, whirling the spoon furiously. "You're going take those ill-gotten gains and lose them all in a card game. Or spend it on some kind of get-rich-quick scheme. Or drink it until it disappears."

"You think that little of me, Calliope?"

Callie stopped stirring and looked at him. In the fading daylight she could see the hurt in his eyes. She sighed and sat back down and wiped her eyes, remorse filtering through her. "Eli, I'm sorry. It's just that I'm . . ." She couldn't admit she was tired. And sore. And frustrated. Not unless she wanted to hear Eli say, 'I told you so' for the next three days.

Without a word he stacked up the firewood into a neat pile. She expected him to grab his bottle of whiskey he'd been working on earlier today and head into the woods, but he didn't. Instead he hunkered down in front of her.

"You're tired, ain't ya?" he asked softly.

Silently she nodded, a lump in her throat, the tears threatening to spill again. She'd insulted him, wounded his pride, yet he treated her with kindness.

"Tell ya what, you go lay down for a spell. Now, don't worry 'bout supper, I'll finish up the stew. I made some mean vittles back in my day."

Relief flooded her. She threw her arms around his shoulder and hugged him tight. He returned it for the briefest of moments, then pushed her away.

"Now, now, don't get all sloppy on me. You run along."

"Thank you, Eli." She kissed his grizzled cheek, something she hadn't done in months,

although she used to do it every night when she
was growing up.

"And I reckon we could head on to Sacramentey in the morning, too, seein' as that's the
nearest big town."

Callie grinned, feeling as if a weight had
been lifted from her shoulders. In Sacramento
they could find a doctor, medicine, clothes—
everything they and the stranger needed.

She squeezed Eli's muscular arm lightly,
then rose. Without looking back she headed
into the cart and climbed in. After a quick
check on the sleeping man, she stretched out
beside him, and fell into the first peaceful sleep
she'd had in a long time.

Chapter Seven

By nightfall Callie and Eli had arrived on the outskirts of Sacramento. They pitched camp in the soft light of dusk, but only unpacked the essentials. Early in the morning they would ride into town and head straight to a doctor.

Callie filled up a small jug with water and carried it into the cart. She sidled alongside the stranger, lit a small oil lamp, and knelt next to him. For a short while she studied his face. The swelling had gone down considerably, revealing a finely-featured man. A tickling sensation flitted around in her belly as she examined him more closely. His eyelashes were long and thick, resting on the top of his cheeks as he slept. Although they were mostly obscured by

73

his unruly beard, she could still make out his full lips.

She imagined what he might have looked like before he'd been beaten and practically starved. She surmised he'd been a muscular but lean man, one who worked outside and enjoyed it. By the singular devotion of his dog, she knew he was kind to animals. Slowly, and with more gumption than she thought she had, she grasped his hand and lifted it up. Dirty, broken fingernails. Calluses. Long scratches and scars on the skin. No doubt from mining gold.

A little stab of guilt pricked at her as she gently released his hand and moved to touch his hair. She was taking advantage of him sleeping, but she couldn't help herself. When had she ever been this close to a man before? Eli didn't count. Sudden stirrings and longings surfaced within her, emotions that confused and pleased her at the same time.

Lightly she ran her palm against his hair. It was a tangled mess, yet it still attracted her. The curls reached down past his shoulders, and she wondered what it would look like clean and combed. She closed her eyes and thought—

"Hey!"

Her eyes flew open and she jerked back her hand. A heated flush seemed to start in her toes and crawl mercilessly up her body as she met his green eyes. They were hooded and half-open, but they also narrowed slightly.

In a scratchy, rough voice he asked sharply, "What are you doing?"

"I-I—" Callie stuttered, moving to put more space between them but finding her back immediately against the wall in the confined cart. She'd managed to move about two inches total.

His gaze moved from hers to the top of the cart, then he looked around, his eyes opening a little wider as he scrutinized his surroundings. "Where am I?" he whispered, almost as if to himself. Then he slowly turned his head toward her, wincing as he did. "And who are you?"

"Callie," she squeaked, appalled that she sounded more like a baby mouse than a woman. Then she cleared her throat. "You're here with me and Eli. We found you two days ago lying on the road. You were nearly dead."

He nodded and swallowed. She watched with fascination as his Adam's apple bobbed up and down.

"I remember . . . they took everything. My gold, my claim . . ."

She wanted to add his clothes, but thought it prudent not to alert him to the fact that he was lying in front of her in just his underwear.

His face contorted in pain. "My dog—"

"Oh no, your dog's just fine."

His eyes widened. "He is? Samson's okay?"

"His name is Samson? What a nice name, it suits him."

"I want to see him."

His tone took her aback. It wasn't a request, it was a demand, and a rather petulant one. Eli's comment about her taking care of a criminal flitted through her mind, but she mentally batted it away. He was in pain and had just lost everything. He had a right to be a little demanding. She would allow him that.

"I'll get him." Opening the cart doors, she called the dog by his name for the first time. "Samson! Come here boy!"

Samson, who had been lying down near the fire with his head resting on his front paws, perked up immediately. He jumped to his feet and sprinted over, leaping into the cart.

"Samson!" The man smiled as his dog enthusiastically licked his face.

Callie's heart stilled. The stranger had a devastating smile. Even through a tangle of beard she could see the beauty of it.

"I'm so glad you're okay," he said to Samson, his voice still gravely and shaky. "I couldn't take it if they had done something to you."

Callie smiled. She couldn't help it. And any doubts she'd harbored about this man instantly vanished. No one who cherished his dog like that could be cruel.

After he'd been sufficiently reacquainted with his canine companion, he turned to Callie. "What did you say your name is again?"

"Callie," she said, her smile dimming a little. Then she remembered the jug of water she'd brought in earlier. "I brought you something to drink."

"Thanks." He accepted the cup she offered to him, although he still eyed her suspiciously. She sought to put him at ease. "We're just outside Sacramento. Tomorrow morning me and Eli—"

"Who's Eli?"

"He's, well, he's Eli. Anyway, we'll go into town and get you to a doctor."

"I don't need a doctor." To her surprise he lifted his head and upper body further than she thought possible. He had to be in pain but he hid it well. "I need to get back to my claim."

"You can't. And you really should lie down." She reached to assist him back down but he shrugged her off.

"Look, I appreciate you and this Eli person helping me, but I'm fine now." He rose to a sitting position, his hair tumbling down his back.

She could hear him stifling his groans, but he still wouldn't lie back down. *Stubborn man.*

"You're not fine," she said, moving so she could talk to his face instead of his back. "You've got a broken arm, bruises all over the place—"

"My claim," he gasped, clearly in pain now.

"You can't get to your claim if you can barely move. Now lay down!"

Breathing heavily, he peered up at her. "My claim," he said weakly.

"You don't need to worry about that right now. Just concentrate on getting well. You almost died back there on that road."

"Maybe it would have been better if I had."

His matter-of-fact tone and the flat expression in his eyes frightened her. "How can you say that? Who would take care of Samson if you had?"

They both turned and looked at the dog who

was sitting up and staring at them out of his one eye, his tongue lolling out of his mouth.

The man let out a deep breath, all of his bluster seemingly sucked right out of him. "God, this hurts."

"Then lie back down," Callie said, her own ire fading. "Here, let me help you." She placed a supporting hand against his thin back and assisted him down. His eyes were tightly shut, his chest heaving.

"I've got something that will help you," she said, reaching for the jug. She poured some water into it and added a bit of white powder. "It will take away the pain." She held it for him as he drank the medicine down.

"You never did tell me your name," she said, placing the empty cup next to the jug.

He licked his lips. "Jeremiah," he said weakly. "Jeremiah Jackson."

Another good name—strong like she knew this man was, both in spirit and in temper. She no longer worried that he wouldn't recover.

His eyes closed and his breathing lightened. She leaned against the cart and sighed. She had thought it would be easier to care for him once he was awake. Now she wasn't so sure.

"Callie?"

He whispered her name so softly she barely heard it. His eyes were still closed as he spoke. She leaned forward to hear the rest of his words.

"Thank you," he said, then drifted off to sleep.

Her lips formed a tiny smile, and again she braved touching him and placed her finger lightly on his brow, smoothing it a little. "You're welcome, Jeremiah Jackson."

Chapter Eight

Jeremiah awoke to the sound of arguing. A man and a woman from what he could tell, although the voices were muffled through the walls of the cart.

"Give 'em back to me!" the man shouted.

"No," the woman replied. "I'm keeping them. Like I said before, we need food, clothing, medicine . . . then there's the doctor to pay."

Doctor? As his fuzzy thoughts became clear, he remembered what happened earlier. Someone named Callie had brought him here, and she wanted to take him to a doctor. He recoiled at the thought and tried to sit up.

"Tarnation, gal!" the man continued. "Ya gonna be the death of me, ya know it? All I'm wantin' is a little bit. It's mine, ya know. I won it, fair and square."

"Eli." Her tone was filled with reproach.

"Okay, unfair and unsquare but its still mine. Not yours to go squander on frilly feminine stuff."

"Since when have I ever bought anything frilly?"

Jeremiah surprised himself by smiling. The argument was kind of amusing.

"Don't rightly recall," Eli continued, "but I'm tellin' you for the last time, missy, give me my gold!"

Samson barked, and Jeremiah realized his dog wasn't still in the cart with him. Samson had never left his side before. But there he was, out there with the two strangers, yipping and yapping and sounding . . . happy. At least as happy as a dog could sound.

Jeremiah tried rising up, but the shooting pain in his arm and torso made him lay back down. He shut his eyes, not only against the pain, but the despair that was welling within him. He was stuck here. He had nothing left, no money, not even clothes. His claim was gone, his gold; the thought of starting all over again made him want to sink back into a deep, dark abyss, never to resurface. He tuned out their squabbling voices as melancholy washed over him in thick, suffocating waves. *They should have just left me. They should have just let me die.*

"Eli, I'm tired of arguing with you!" She shoved the bags of gold deeper into the pockets of her apron and curved her hands around it.

"If you'd start respectin' yer elders like yer supposed to, we wouldn't be fightin'!" He clenched his meaty hands into fists and came stalking toward her. "By my Aunt Gussy's grave—"

"You never had an Aunt Gussy." Callie didn't move, just kept her grip on the precious gold. Eli had been right about one thing—they wouldn't have to worry about money for a long time. As long as she kept control of it, that is. It had been easy to get the pouches from him as he soundly slept last night. Now that she had them in her possession she wasn't going to let them go, not until after they had spent as much as they needed on supplies first, along with a visit to the doctor. Eli had been in charge of their money before, and it had been disastrous.

She glanced at the tinker's cart and thought about Jeremiah again. It was well into morning, and she had expected him to have at least stirred. But she hadn't heard anything from him since sunup. Concerned, she turned from Eli. "I need to check on Jeremiah."

"Shore, use him as a 'scuse to get away," Eli spat. He trailed right behind her as she went to the wagon. "I'm tellin' ya gal, one way or 'nother I'm gettin' what's due to me. You ain't gonna control my destnee, that's for shore. Whew! Lawdy, it smells plum awful in there!"

Cassie took an involuntary step back from the open doors of the cart. Her nose scrunched. Eli was right, the whole cart reeked of stale blood, dirty dog, and filthy man. Jeremiah certainly couldn't stay in the cart much longer—it definitely needed airing out.

Catching her breath, she stepped forward. "Jeremiah?"

He didn't move at first. After a few long moments she saw him open his eyes, then shield them with his hand from the brightness of the intruding sunlight. His groan was plainly audible.

"Well, would you look at that?" a short, stocky man remarked, peering inside the wagon. Eli, Jeremiah assumed. As his eyes adjusted he could make out his wizened face, rounded nose, and broad shoulders. Jeremiah could also see Samson sitting on the ground behind him.

Callie appeared next. She was a little taller than Eli, with rounded shoulders that seemed to point inward a little. He hadn't noticed it until that moment.

"I'll be a buffalo's uncle," Eli continued. "Your young man's alive!"

"Of course he's alive," she hissed. "And he's *not* my young man." She turned to Jeremiah, her gaze searching. "How are you feeling?"

It felt like flames were licking up and down his broken arm. His other arm shook as he held it up as a barrier to the light. "How do you think I'm feeling?" he snapped. Then he let out a deep sigh. "Just leave me alone."

"Yep," Eli muttered, clearly disgusted. "He was worth savin' alright."

Callie didn't say anything for a moment. Straightening her shoulders, which really didn't amount to much straightening at all, she lifted her chin. "I'm sorry we disturbed you. I need to start on breakfast." She whirled on her heel, and moved over to the small fire several feet away from the cart, her back remaining hunched over.

Jeremiah looked at Eli. The old man spit on the ground and stared back at him. "Boy," he said, his tone dark, "You can say what ya want 'bout me, I don't give a lick. If I'd had my druthers you'd be dead in the mountains, and me an' Callie would be on our way to Coloradey. But no, she wanted to *save* you, 'cause she's a kindhearted soul. An' you hurt her jest now. So if you eva, eva, *eva* say 'nother harsh word to my Callie, you'll regret it." He moved over to the side of the cart and out of view for a second, then came back, a beat up pot in his hand. He tossed it at Jeremiah, almost hitting him in the chest.

"What's this for?"

"I 'spect you got some personal business to attend to, seeing you been cooped up for over a day. But that," he gestured to the pot, "is the only help you're gettin' from me." With that he slammed the cart door shut, leaving Jeremiah alone in the dark.

Half an hour later Callie pounded on the biscuit dough with her hand as Eli and Samson headed for the nearby creek to catch some fish. Resentment fueled inside her. She tried to remind herself that Jeremiah was in pain, that he'd lost everything. Still, he didn't have to be so snappish with her. How could she have been so wrong about that man? He might know how to treat his dog, but he had no idea how to relate to a fellow human being.

As she folded and kneaded the dough on a smooth wooden board in her lap, her anger and frustration increased. He should be kissing her feet for all she'd done for him: bathed his wounds, set his arm, gave both him and his smelly dog her sleeping place. She'd treated him with nothing but kindness—

She stilled, her fingers stuck in the dough. Was that really why she'd taken care of Jeremiah? So he could be in her debt? So she could lord it over him when he healed? So she could feel self-important? She thought back to the day they'd found him. Those thoughts hadn't even crossed her mind; at the time all she could think about was making sure he didn't die.

So if she hadn't expected his unwavering and infinite gratitude, then why did she want it so badly?

Chapter Nine

Jeremiah lay in the darkness, his thoughts whirling around inside his head. They had done what he'd asked them to do—they left him alone, alone and feeling like a first class heel.

Callie's hurt expression played over and over in his mind. He'd had no right to snap at her that way, frustrated or not. Regardless of his circumstances, she had saved his life. And whether or not he agreed at the moment that he deserved saving, she had done it, and apparently wasn't expecting anything in return, since he had nothing to give.

Slowly he sat up, pain shooting through his body. But he remained undeterred. An apology was what Callie deserved, and an apology was what she was going to get.

Callie had just finished shaping the last biscuit when she heard the sound of the cart doors flinging open. She watched in fascination as one skinny leg poked out of the cart, then the other. Finally Jeremiah appeared, holding his broken arm against his chest, the brightness of calico contrasting with his ash-colored skin. His bare toes touched the top step of the short ladder that was at the bottom of the cart.

When he moved to stand on his wobbly legs, she couldn't stay there any longer. All her resentment toward him dissipated, replaced by pity as she watched him struggle. She knocked the biscuit dough to the ground and hurried over to him, holding him up just as he was about to fall down, her arm going around his thin waist.

"Are you daft?" she admonished, looking up at him, way up. With him standing on the top step, he seemed like a skinny giant.

"I thought if I could—"

"You thought if you could sit you could stand, and if you could stand you could walk."

"Right," he said, sounding surprised.

"I guess you found out it doesn't work that way. You should have just asked me to help you." She tried to ignore the tingling sensation in the tips of her fingers as they pressed against his bare skin. He really needed to get some clothes.

"After what I've done and said, I don't have the right to ask you for anything."

She paused, his response surprising her. It wasn't cloaked in sarcasm or resentment. It was a simple statement of fact.

Then she became aware of his body shaking. From cold or fatigue she didn't know, but he needed to sit down. "Lean on me. We'll go over by the fire."

He did, and the heaviness of him was almost too much for her to bear. He might be thin, but he was tall and almost dead weight. Somehow they managed to navigate the steps together and make it over to her small stool.

Gingerly he sat down, then nodded his thanks. He looked up at her, his eyes round and hollow, but filled with gratitude. His complexion was pale beneath the yellowing bruises on his face.

As they always seemed to do around him, Callie's emotions warred within her. How could she remain upset with him when he looked at her like that? She could read the apology in his eyes before he said anything.

"I'm sorry." He shifted on the stool but never broke eye contact with her. "I should have never spoken to you like that."

"It's alright—"

"No, it's not. I don't know what got into me."

A breeze kicked up. Although it was warm, it made Jeremiah shiver. He glanced down at his ripped up long johns and bare feet, as if seeing himself for the first time. "They really did take everything," he muttered.

"Let me get you a blanket. After breakfast I'll give you some of Eli's clothes." She went to the cart and pulled out an old quilt. It was well worn, but it was soft and good at trapping warmth. Coming up behind him, she draped it over his shoulders, her hands involuntarily lingering a moment longer than they should have.

Her cheeks hot, she looked away, grateful his back was to her. But in the next second he turned around, an odd expression on his face. "Thanks," he said.

"You're welcome." Unable to look directly at him, she gathered up the ruined biscuit dough and kneading board and clutched them to her.

"Sorry about breakfast too," he said.

"Not to worry." Staring straight down at the ground she rushed past him. "I can make more."

"Give the dough to Samson. He'll appreciate the treat."

She did as he instructed, tossing the dough to the dog, who immediately began wolfing it down. Retrieving more flour, lard, and water from their diminishing supplies, she sat down on the ground next to the cart and made fresh biscuits, still trying to sort out her myriad of emotions concerning Jeremiah.

"I don't bite."

She looked up from her kneading board. "What?"

He turned around slowly, looking at her over his shoulder. "What's that old saying, 'his bark is worse than his bite'? That's true about me too."

"I-I think I'll stay over here just the same." Her voice was tiny again, like some skittering little chipmunk or something.

He turned back around. "Suit yourself."

Her palms grew damp as she watched him, even though her hands were covered in flour. *What was wrong with her? Why was she nervous all of a sudden?*

Eli emerged from the woods, three small fish

hanging from a string, a makeshift fishing rod over his shoulder. Samson trailed behind. Eli cast Jeremiah a scathing look and plopped the fish on the ground.

"Here ya go, Callie. Breakfast is served."

She quickly finished shaping her biscuits and went to the fire. At least with Eli here she could focus on fixing breakfast, and not on the man who kept on thoroughly throwing her thoughts and feelings into a tailspin.

Chapter Ten

Jeremiah's stomach growled at the delicious aroma of fish frying on a spit over the fire. He watched in silence as Callie deftly prepared the meal. He still couldn't believe what a complete fool he'd been to her. Yet here she was, helping him sit down. Getting a blanket for him when he shivered. Fixing him breakfast. And all without complaint or resentment. He didn't know what to make of her.

In the light of morning he had a much clearer view of her than he'd had in the dimness of the cart. Her slumped shoulders made her appear much older than the smooth skin of her face revealed her to be. Her brown dress had a high neck, one that reached almost to her chin. She wore her brown hair in a thick braid down her back.

"When's them vittles gonna be done, gal?"

Jeremiah shifted his attention to Eli, observing the man reclining against a large rock, picking at the dirt under his fingernails. Jeremiah's pity turned to irritation. Couldn't he see she was working as fast as she could? Better yet, why couldn't he get off his rear and help put the meal together?

"In a minute." She shuffled over to the spit and checked on it. "The fish is almost done."

"Good, 'cause I'm hungry." He looked up from his hand and eyed Jeremiah, who was still watching him. "What you lookin' at?"

Jeremiah's gaze didn't waver. "I was wondering the same thing."

Eli's expression was stony, and for a split second Jeremiah thought the man was going to jump to his feet and challenge him to a fight. And Eli would win too; Jeremiah didn't have the strength to fight a mosquito, much less a man.

Then, surprisingly, Eli chuckled. "This one's got spunk, Calliope. You ain't got to worry 'bout him no more. He's gonna be fine."

Jeremiah looked at Callie and saw her cheeks

turn bright red. "I'm not worried about him, Eli," she said, her focus squarely on the sizzling fish.

"Oh, yes, you are." He got up and walked over to Jeremiah, and sat down beside him. "You should have seen her, fussin' over ya, givin' up her medicine, her place to sleep. Heck, she wouldn't leave yer side for hours after we picked ya up off the road."

"Eli!" Callie stood. "That's enough."

But Jeremiah could see she was already thoroughly embarrassed. If her face grew any redder, it would explode. Feeling the need to alleviate her discomfort, he tried to put her at ease. "I appreciate you taking care of me."

"Hmph," Eli said. "You didn't sound too 'preciative before."

"I was an idiot."

"You ain't gettin' no argument from me on that count, boy."

Callie remained silent, turning her attention back to the fish. She stared at it for a long time.

"Calliope!" Eli jumped up and grabbed one of the ends of the spit. "Ow! That dadburn thing is hot."

"Then what did you grab it for?" Callie said, clearly annoyed with him for interfering.

"You were lettin' the fish burn, that's why! Where's your head, gal?"

"I had everything under control." But her tone was doubtful. "Now give that back."

He handed it to her. "Burned meself," he muttered, sucking on his fingers.

Jeremiah watched and listened as they bickered again, as if he were no longer there. He wondered about their relationship—Eli was obviously many years older than her. Old enough to be her father and then some, he figured. Yet if he was her father, why did she call him by his first name? She would call him dad—even uncle if he was a relative.

Callie suddenly appeared in front of him, a plate in her hands. He looked up at her as he accepted the fish. This close to her he could see her eyes, which weren't just one single color, but a myriad of browns, golds, and greens.

"You are hungry, aren't you?"

Her question brought him out of his thoughts. "Um, yes," he replied, taking the plate. Now it was his turn to be embarrassed, getting caught staring at her so intently.

Picking up her own plate she went and sat next to Eli, who was already polishing off his own breakfast. "Eat slowly," she advised.

It took Jeremiah a second to realize she was talking to him, not Eli. Still, he ignored her advice. His stomach churned with hunger, and he attacked his meal like it was still alive and about to escape off his plate. After the third big mouthful he groaned as his belly recoiled.

She immediately rose and went to him, and started to remove his plate from his lap. "That's enough."

"Aw, let the man eat, Calliope."

"Eli, if he eats too much he'll get sick. He's not used to having a lot of food. Look how thin he is."

"I'm fine," Jeremiah said, hanging on to the plate. He didn't appreciate being talked about as if he wasn't there. Plus, despite his rebelling stomach, he was still hungry.

"Jeremiah—" she said, tugging on the plate.

"Callie—" He pulled back. The plate suddenly flipped out of his hands, and in a flash Samson was there, lapping it all up.

Eli laughed. "Serves ya right," he said, wiping his chin with his sleeve. "Fightin' over food like ya both are barely out of the cradle." He stood, leaving his empty plate on the ground. "I gotta make a visit to the bushes." With that announcement he headed away from the camp.

Samson immediately followed. It seemed the dog had found a new friend. For some odd reason Jeremiah was glad for that.

"I'm sorry," Callie said. "That was my fault."

Before he could reply she turned away and went to the stool where she'd been sitting. "Here," she said, handing him her nearly full plate. "Have mine."

As tempting as the food was, he couldn't accept it. It was more than obvious she and Eli didn't feast like kings, and they had wasted enough food that morning. "No, you were right. I shouldn't have eaten so fast."

She regarded him for a moment, those amazing eyes of hers seemingly changing color as she tilted her head to the side. Then she went and got her stool and sat beside him. "We'll share."

They ate in silence for a few moments. Once their hands touched as they both reached for a biscuit, but she snatched hers away, as if his skin was on fire.

"After breakfast we'll break camp and head for town," she said, looking down at her lap. She pinched off a tiny piece of biscuit. "We'll go straight to the doctor's and have him take a look at you."

"Callie—"

"I know what you're going to say." She looked at him. "You need a doctor. And we have the money. For once," she added quietly.

"I'll pay you back," he said. "I don't know how, but I will."

Her lips curved into a smile. "I know you will."

Jeremiah smiled back. He couldn't help it. Not only was her smile contagious, it transformed her face from plain to . . . pretty. Very pretty. And as he looked at her, he realized what an amazing person she truly was. Not everyone would have stopped to help a complete stranger, much less put that stranger's needs before her own. But she did, willingly, and seemingly without expecting anything in return. His smile faded. She instantly noticed.

"Jeremiah? Is something wrong?"

"Why did you do it?"

She appeared puzzled by his question. "Do what?"

"Stop and help me. Brought me with you. You could have just left me there, but you didn't."

Callie stared down at her lap, her fingers entwining with each other. "You were hurt. I couldn't have lived with myself if I'd just walked away."

"Callie!"

Jeremiah's head jerked up at the sound of Eli's screaming voice. Callie rose from her seat as the man emerged from the cluster of trees nearby, Samson right behind. She hurried toward him. "Eli? What's wrong?"

"They've found us. Dang blasted fools found us." Hastily he started grabbing things willy-nilly. "We gots to go, gal. Pack up and head out."

"How do you know?"

"I jest know! Now don't argy with me gal!"

Jeremiah watched in bewilderment as Callie immediately joined him in gathering up their belongings. "Who found us? What are you talking about?"

"Never you mind 'bout that." He kicked dirt over the fire. "Sorry, Calliope, but we can't go to Sacramentey now."

"Then where are we going?" she asked as she grabbed up their dishes and put them in a small metal washtub.

"Anywhere but here, gal." Eli looked at Jeremiah. "Well don't just sit there like yer a bump on a dadburn log, get movin'. We ain't got much time."

With more strength than he thought he had, Jeremiah stood up. His legs were steadier than before, but he still moved slowly toward the cart. He glanced around as Eli and Callie haphazardly started tossing things inside. He should be helping them. Instead it was all he could do to put one foot in front of the other. The blanket that had been around his shoulders slid to the ground.

"For Pete's sake, Calliope go help him. We'll be here forever an' a day at the rate he's goin'."

She appeared at his side, sliding her arm around his waist for support. "Lean on me, just like you did before."

Her touch was soft, yet strong at the same time, her hand warm on his skin. He did as she instructed, confident that despite her slight frame, she wouldn't let him fall. As quickly as he could he moved to the cart, then climbed inside.

Callie looked at him. "I've got to help Eli—"

"I'm fine," Jeremiah insisted. He leaned back against the bedroll, surprisingly winded from the short journey. "Go on. I'll be okay."

A smile teased at her lips for a brief instant, then she disappeared. Jeremiah lay down, his chest rising and falling with each breath he took. His mind raced almost as fast. Callie and Eli were on the run. But from who? They could be running from anyone—the law, or scoundrels,

Chapter Eleven

"Are you sure it was them, Eli?"

Eli unhitched the mules from a nearby tree. "Why are you questionin' me, gal? My gut ain't steered me wrong yet, and it ain't about to start doin' it now."

Callie blew a stray strand of hair from her face. "But did you see them?"

"No, I didn't see them!" He turned and scowled at her. "I didn't have to see them. I sensed them. An' they ain't far from here, so you get in the back right this minute. The dog too. An' keep quiet back there. I don't wanna alert 'em that we're here."

Knowing he was serious, Callie acquiesced. She and Samson climbed into the cart as Eli slapped the reins on the team. When the cart lurched forward, she lost her balance, and fell on top of Jeremiah.

"Oof," he exclaimed as her head hit him square in the chest, but fortunately away from his broken arm.

"I said keep quiet!" Eli barked.

Callie rolled off Jeremiah. "I'm sorry," she whispered, trying to position herself next to him without actually touching him, which was proving impossible. And embarrassing, now that he was fully conscious and they'd actually had a few conversations. She continued to fidget, her face heating with each passing second. When she tried to sit up, her head hit a low hung pot suspended from the ceiling.

"Wait." Jeremiah's voice was low, barely audible above the din of the rolling cart and plodding mules. He raised his good arm parallel to his shoulder, giving her more room. "Lay down here."

She shook her head vehemently. "I couldn't possibly—"

"Callie don't be ridiculous. You can't ride hunched over like that."

He was right, she couldn't. Her back was already screaming in pain.

"I'll be a perfect gentleman, I promise. You can trust me."

"I know." But could she trust herself not to see the situation for more than it was; they were trying to make themselves as comfortable as possible while stuck in a cramped space. She focused on that as she straightened out beside him, laying her head on his shoulder. She balled her hands into fists and tucked them underneath her chin, the rest of her body remaining rigid and stiff. She heard Samson settle at their feet.

"Can I put my hand here?"

"What?" she blurted, a little too loudly. Then a little more quietly she repeated, "What?"

"Here." Lightly he dropped his hand to her shoulder. She could feel his muscles shaking underneath her cheek. He wouldn't have been able to hold his arm up much longer.

"Y-yes, um, that's fine."

"Okay. I think we're all set then."

They lay there for a few moments, the motion of the cart calming her nerves a bit, but not much. And definitely not enough to keep her from thinking about touching his long curly beard that was now at her eye level. Or preventing her from realizing how safe and secure she felt with his arm around her shoulders, even though it was out of necessity and nothing more. Warmth pooled in her belly and slowly spread throughout her body. She closed her eyes and her imagination began to take flight.

Jeremiah felt Callie's body relax next to him. "Callie?"

"Hmm?" she murmured. "Oh, I mean yes?"

"Who's chasing us?"

He felt her tense. "I don't know."

She was lying. "I don't believe you."

A pause. "Then that's your choice."

"Callie—"

"Shhh. We have to be quiet."

"Callie," he whispered this time. "You've got to tell me what's going on."

She sighed, relaxing again. "Alright. I can tell you what I know at least. Eli got caught cheating at cards, so the men he swindled are after us. That's basically it."

Jeremiah remembered Callie and Eli's argument earlier that morning. "I take it he got some gold off of them."

"Yes, quite a bit. But I'm not pleased about how he obtained it. I don't condone cheating."

"I didn't think you would."

"Eli, unfortunately, doesn't have a problem with it. And his intentions are good, most of the time."

The cart suddenly hit a large bump. Instinctively Jeremiah's arm tightened around Callie, his hand cupping her shoulder. Beneath the fabric of her dress he felt something ridged and bumpy. Without thinking he ran his fingers lightly over it.

She sprang up to a sitting position. "Don't!" Hugging her knees to her chest, she wrapped her arms around them.

He rose up on one elbow. "Callie—"

"Don't touch me again."

Jeremiah searched her face, but she turned away from him. The hurt in her tone pierced him inside. "Callie . . ."

She didn't respond. She didn't even look at him. Instead she remained in that crouched position, her head on her knees facing the back of the cart.

He lay back down, his fingers still tingling from the contact with her shoulder, still remembering the strange bumps that protruded slightly through the fabric. But more than that, he felt cold. And oddly empty. He wanted to beckon her to lie back down, to be more comfortable. To let him hold her again. Yet he knew better than to ask. It was obvious she'd shut down completely.

Her reaction was one more piece of the ever growing puzzle that was Callie Winters.

Callie wanted to shrivel up and die.

Tears came to her eyes, but she squeezed them back. How could she have been so careless? She'd allowed herself to become too close to him; to think about things she had no business thinking about, like touching him and holding him close . . . until he'd felt what she always kept hidden from the world.

Wool and cotton could cover it, but not make it disappear. That fact was driven home when his fingers had trailed over her shoulder.

She knew he'd felt it. Now he would be repulsed, just like everyone else who saw her. A rock hard lump formed in her throat, and she couldn't swallow it down.

"Callie."

He called her name again, but she ignored him. She had to pretend he wasn't there, lying beside her. She had to forget what his nearness did to her emotions, how the sound of his voice affected her. She had to disregard it all in order keep her heart in one piece.

But try as she could, she couldn't blank out the memories. They came upon her like a suffocating cloak, threatening to rob the very breath from her body. Screwing her eyes shut, she steeled herself against their painful onslaught.

"Mommy, mommy, it burns!"

"It will take a long time to heal, maybe months."

"I can't stand to look at her . . . she's hideous!"

"Mommy? Mommy? Why won't my mommy come to see me?"

So many voices; so many images and so much pain. The tears escaped this time, trailing down her cheeks in streaky rivulets. Involuntarily she sniffed, trying to hold it all in.

"Callie?"

She heard him move next to her; sensed him sitting, his body curving forward in order to avoid those annoying hanging pots and pans.

"Are you crying?"

Her only answer was another helpless sniff.

"Talk to me, Callie. Please."

Slowly she turned to him. "You wouldn't understand."

Even in the dim light of the cart she could see the kindness in his eyes. "Try me."

She wanted to—more than anything she wanted to explain what was wrong. "I can't," she said, wiping the back of her hand across her face.

"Okay." He paused for a moment. "How about a trade then?"

"Trade?"

"I'll tell you something about me, and you tell me something about you in return. That way its fair and we'll get to know each other a little better. Plus we have to pass the time somehow. After all, it looks like we're going to be cooped up in here for a while. Eli seems bent on getting us out of here."

"He is. I just hope the mules can take the pace."

"I think they will. I can tell they're hardy animals."

"You know a lot about animals, don't you?"

"Yep. I was raised on a ranch." He lay back down, his good arm behind his head for support. "A sheep ranch, to be exact."

"Really? I've never been on a farm. Where is it?"

"You won't find that out until you tell me something about you."

She smiled, and was surprised she was capable of it. With a few words and a kind look he was able to bring her out of her misery, and she was grateful for it.

Chapter Twelve

"So I have to tell you something about me," Callie said thoughtfully.

"That's how the game works," Jeremiah replied.

"We're playing a game?"

"I guess you could call it that." He settled his arm against his chest, glad she was talking. A few moments ago he wasn't sure if she would ever speak to him again. Her reaction to his touching her had alarmed him, and he didn't want to upset her anymore than he already had. So if playing a "game" was what it took for her to trust him again, he would do it willingly.

"How old are you?" he asked, starting with something simple.

"Twenty-four," she replied. "And you?"

"Twenty."

"Oh. I didn't realize I was that much older than you."

"Well, age is just a number anyway. Where are you from?"

She grew reticent again. "Here and there."

"Sounds like an interesting place," he said dryly.

"Trust me, its not. I'd much rather we find a town and settle down. I'm tired of traveling. Eli and I have been doing it for so long."

"Then Eli's your father?"

Callie shook her head.

"Uncle?"

She shrugged. "Eli's, just . . . Eli. I've known him since I was a little girl."

"How did you two meet?"

"Wait a minute." She unclasped her hands, which had been wrapped around her legs. "I think you owe me an answer to a question or two."

"I reckon you're right. Ask away."

Touching her finger to her chin, she spoke. "Where's your ranch?"

"Texas. San Antonio, to be precise."

A slight frown formed on her lips. "That's really far from here."

You have no idea. "I left a year ago, to make my fortune in the gold mines." He gestured to himself. "Some fortune."

"It wasn't your fault you were robbed."

"No, but if I hadn't left home in the first place . . ." A tugging sensation pulled on his heart, the same one that always appeared when he thought of home.

"Do you have any brothers or sisters?"

"Two. One died at the Alamo, along with my father. He was the oldest. Then there's Luke. He's married with four kids. They're all staying at the ranch with Ma now."

Callie smiled. "That sounds wonderful—a family, a home. You're very lucky to have that."

Her words yanked harder on his emotions. "But I don't have it anymore. When I left, I didn't even say good-bye." He frowned, surprised he was admitting this to her. Yet it was a relief to talk about it. "I can't ever go back again."

"Why not?"

"They wouldn't want me. Not after what I'd done."

She grew very, very quiet. "I know what that's like," she finally whispered.

"To hurt your family? I doubt you could ever do something like that, Callie."

"No, not that. I know what its like to be unwanted." She averted her gaze.

He sat up and moved closer to her. Reaching out his hand, he touched her arm with his finger. She shrugged him off.

"Who did this to you, Callie? Who hurt you?"

She opened her mouth to speak when the wagon suddenly lurched forward to a stop.

"Calliope!" Eli shouted. "Get out and help me, gal!"

"Coming!" Quickly she scooted to the end of the cart and opened the doors. Casting a stark glance at Jeremiah, she then clambered out of the cart along with Samson and disappeared.

But not before he saw her wince as she moved. And not before he heard her muffled moan as she stood up, her posture remaining stooped.

Something had happened to her, something that caused her great pain. The mere thought of it tore him up inside. *How had he grown to care so much for her in such a short time?* The feelings he had went beyond gratitude. They gave him strength, and the impetus to get back on his feet as soon as possible. He had hindered them both long enough.

Chapter Thirteen

"They ain't gonna find us here, Calliope."

Callie surveyed the area. Eli had managed to find a very secluded spot, surrounded by tall, thick trees and clumps of stocky bushes. She could hear the faint rush of water, indicating a stream nearby. The clearing was big enough for their cart, the horses, and a small campfire. Like everything else in her life, it was cramped and temporary.

"Get started on dinner," Eli ordered. "I'm so hungry I could eat a bear."

"How long have we been traveling?"

"Too long, Calliope." Eli rubbed his rump. "Too long. I figure its late afternoon at least." He grabbed his slingshot from the buckseat.

119

"I'm gonna have a look 'round. Be back lickety-split." Whistling for Samson, they both headed into the woods.

"Looks like Samson's found a friend."

Callie whirled around to see Jeremiah standing, albeit swaying a little, in front of her. "How—"

"Seems you got the healing touch." He adjusted the sling around his broken arm. "About those clothes you mentioned this morning . . ."

"Oh, yes, of course." She went to the back of the cart and rummaged inside it for a moment. Pulling out an old flannel shirt and a pair of nearly threadbare trousers, she handed them to him. "I know they're not much, but it's all we have right now."

"They'll be fine." He held up the pants. "But these don't look like Eli's."

"They're not. They belong to the tinker who used to own the cart. I thought they might fit you better, since you're so tall."

Jeremiah raised a brow. "Dare I ask how you came about separating the tinker from his livelihood?"

"Dice," Callie replied. Then she sighed. "Loaded dice."

He chuckled. "I'm not surprised." Scanning

the small clearing, he asked, "Is there a creek nearby?"

"Sounds like it."

"Good. I need a bath. Hate to dirty up these clean clothes."

"I'll get you some soap." A few seconds later she returned with a decent-sized brown sliver and handed it to him. "Here's a razor, too, if you want to use it."

"Much obliged." His hand went to his fuzzy beard. "I am getting tired of it." Slowly he started walking in the direction of the creek, swaying slightly. Callie followed after him, worried he might fall.

"Do you need some help?" She wanted to bite back the question as soon as she asked it.

With deliberate movements he turned around, a mischievous twinkle in his eye. "Ma'am, while that's by far the best offer I've had all day, I'm afraid I'll have to decline."

His exaggerated Southern drawl made her laugh, sending her initial embarrassment of asking to assist with his bath disappear. He dipped his head toward her once, then turned back around and continued on to the creek.

She watched him leave, although she was still worried about his unsteadiness. But she couldn't keep hovering over him like a mother hen would with her chick.

A twinge of sadness pricked at her, more than a twinge actually. While she wanted him to get better, it also meant he would be leaving soon, probably when they arrived at the next town. There would be no reason for him to stay.

Suddenly she wasn't in such a hurry to find that town anymore.

By the time Jeremiah had returned from the creek she had pulled out some salted beef and a few leftover biscuits from breakfast. She didn't dare set a fire, in case their pursuers saw the smoke, but she did light a small lantern and hung it from the outside hook on the side of the cart.

From afar she could see his hair was wet, hanging in thick strands that almost reached his elbows. With the curls stretched out, she couldn't believe how long it was. The clothes were the right size for his height, but too roomy for his frame, and she could see he had cinched the belt on the last hole. He was looking down as he walked, taking care not to step on anything that might cause him to stumble. When he was within a few feet from her, he looked up and smiled.

She all but swooned on the spot.

His beard was gone, leaving a gaunt, but devastatingly handsome face behind. She could see his features clearly now: high cheekbones, square jaw, and full, inviting lips.

"Callie? Is everything alright?"

She searched to find her voice. "Why, uh." She cleared her throat. "Why, yes, everything's fine." Turning away from him, she tried to pick up the leftover potato peelings, but discovered her fingers weren't working properly.

"Good. The way you were staring at me, I thought you'd seen a ghost or something."

Hardly. "No, no, not a ghost." She kept her back to him. "Stew okay for lunch?"

"Whatever you fix is fine by me." He came up behind her as she stood. "I wondered if I could ask for one more favor."

"Sure," she said, her voice shaky at his nearness. She could practically feel him breathing behind her.

"Could you cut my hair? I tried getting the knots and tangles out with my fingers, but it's impossible. Better to just get rid of it all together."

Swallowing, she pursed her lips together. "Okay," she said, once she could trust herself to speak. "Let me get my scissors."

"Thanks, Callie. I really appreciate it."

After she retrieved her scissors and a comb, she had him sit down on the stool, then stared at the wild mass of hair.

"How short do you want it?"

He shrugged. "You decide. I trust you."

If only she could trust herself. With a shaky hand she touched a thick, unruly lock, and took a deep breath. This was a mistake, since he smelled like soap and fresh air and a distinctly masculine scent, one that made her toes curl inside her shoes. Absently she drew her hand down the length of his hair, only to draw it back sharply when she realized what she was doing.

He chuckled.

"What's so funny?"

"Nothing," he said. Then he whistled innocently. "Just waiting on you, that's all."

"Okay, I'm getting to it. It's just—"

He turned and faced her. "Just what, Callie?"

Oh, why did he have to be this good looking and this nice? She tried remembering the man that had insulted her only yesterday, but she couldn't. Not when she was this close to him.

His hand closed around hers as she held on to the scissors. "You don't have to do this. I can probably cut it myself."

The image of him trying to cut his own hair

with only one hand flitted through her mind. "Don't be ridiculous, I'll do it. Turn back around."

Jeremiah did as he was told. "Anytime you're ready."

Grabbing a hank of hair, she spread the scissors open. *Stop being such a ninny. You've cut Eli's hair dozens of times. Jeremiah's no different. It's just hair, after all.* But it wasn't just hair. Jeremiah's hair had a different texture, a different feel, and she had kept him waiting long enough. Without further hesitation she cut the chunk off right above his shoulders, and kept cutting until it was an even length all around.

"Feels like I lost ten more pounds," he said when she'd finished with the scissors.

Glancing at the piles of hair on the ground around them, she nodded. "I think you did." Taking the comb, she slid it through the strands until all the residual tangles disappeared. "There. You'll still be able to tie it back if you want to." She moved to stand in front of him. "I just need to see if the sides are even."

He tilted up his chin as she examined her handiwork. "Keep still," she ordered, her hand automatically going to his jaw. It remained there, her palm against the smoothness of his cheek. Without thinking she let her thumb move ever so slightly across it, reveling in the feel of a man's face against her skin. The swelling from the bruises had gone down, and she barely noticed the purple and yellow marks shading his eyes and chin.

"Callie."

His voice was hoarse, but he didn't move. It gave her the courage to stroke him again. He pressed his cheek further into her hand, then reached up and ran the back of his fingers alongside her jaw.

But when she felt his hands move from her face toward her shoulders, she broke away. "No," she said, jerking out of his arms and standing before him. "Don't."

"Callie—"

"I'm sorry," she said, her voice breaking. "I-I can't do this, Jeremiah."

He rose, faster than she thought possible. With his free arm he reached for her. She shied away again. "Why won't you let me touch you?"

"You wouldn't understand—"

"Then explain it to me."

"Jeremiah," she said in a small voice. "Don't. Please."

"Whatever it is, I'll understand. You've got to trust me. I promise. I'm not like that other man."

She furrowed her brows in confusion. "Other man."

"The one that hurt you. That's why you're afraid, right? Why you keep pulling away. You're afraid of getting hurt again."

Unbidden, tears rolled down her cheeks. "If it were only that simple," she whispered, mostly to herself.

"Darlin', I can see that you're in pain. You helped me. Now let me help you."

Maybe it was the gentle way he called her darling in that sweet Southern drawl of his. Or maybe it was the honest sincerity she saw in his eyes. Whatever it was, her hand went unbidden to the top button of her collar. She unfastened it. Then the next one. And the next. She would keep undoing them until she exposed to him what she'd kept secret from the rest of the world, except for Eli. He'd known, and he'd accepted and loved her despite of it.

"Callie," Jeremiah said, moving toward her as his gaze transfixed on her collar.

"You wanted to know why I keep pulling away," she said, unbuttoning the fourth button with trembling fingers. "I'm going to show you."

Chapter Fourteen

Jeremiah closed the gap between them, placing his hand on hers and stilling it. *Is this what she thought he wanted from her?* "What are you doing?"

But she wriggled away from him. "I want you to look, Jeremiah. Look at me." She folded down the sides of her high collar. "Look at me and see if you still want to get close."

Before he could respond she pulled down the bodice of her dress exposing a bare shoulder. What he saw made him speechless.

"This," she said, "is just a small portion." Turning around, she lowered the dress further, revealing her back.

Jeremiah sucked in his breath. Scars, ugly,

rippling ridges of scars covered her back and shoulders. They were narrow in some places, wide in others. Where there was no scarring the skin was stretched taut, keeping her from standing up straight; from ever standing up straight again. "What . . ." he managed to say in a strangled voice.

"Burns." She pulled her dress up and turned around, frantically buttoning it back up as she spoke. "When I was four, one of the servants threw a pan of hot grease out of the kitchen window. She didn't know I was playing with my dolls underneath it."

Gulping, he couldn't keep from staring at her. It all made sense to him now. Eli saying how she gave up her medicine. Sacrificed her sleeping space. Her poor posture, her shuffling steps. Her valiant attempts at hiding her pain.

Her resistance to his touch.

"You don't have to say anything," she said dully. "I can tell by your expression. I've seen that look before, on my mother's face. Before she sent me away."

Jeremiah was stunned. "Your own mother sent you away?"

"She couldn't bear it. Or rather she couldn't bear *me*. She couldn't stand to hear my screams at night when I couldn't sleep. Or see my back when the servants could finally give me a bath. Or even hold me in her arms. I wasn't her little girl anymore. I was this deformed creature she didn't recognize.

"So she sent me to a little town outside of St. Louis. That's where I'm originally from. Can you believe I used to live in a big, sprawling house, right in the heart of the city?" A bitter laugh escaped from her throat. "Far cry from where I live now, isn't it?"

"Callie—"

"I moved in with the sister of one of our maids," she said, not letting him speak. "She was a teacher and a spinster. She taught me how to read and write, how to mind my manners. All the things a little girl needs to know to live in proper society. She had a brother who would come visit every once in a while. He was a drifter, and would show up mostly when he needed money, after one or another of his lousy business deals fell through."

"Eli," Jeremiah supplied.

"Yes. But when I was ten she took ill with fever and died. That's when Eli and I hit the road." She looked away. "We've been hitting it ever since."

Jeremiah didn't know what to say. What could he say? He had offered to help her, but instead he was the one who felt helpless. What could he possibly do to take away the years of rejection and pain Callie lived with?

Regaining her composure, she wiped away the moisture from her eyes and straightened her collar. "I have to see to lunch. Eli will be hungry when he returns." Turning her back to him, she walked over to the meager rations laid out on the cutting board and began arranging them as if nothing unusual had happened between them.

He stood there, unsure of what to do next, still trying to comprehend what she'd told him, what she'd shown him. The impact of it blew into him like a gale force wind, knocking him off balance. Slowly he lowered himself onto the stool.

She didn't turn around. She didn't speak. She simply shut him out . . . again.

"Whooo wee, we're gonna be eatin' good!"

Eli appeared carrying two squirrels by the tail. "I'm telling ya, Jeremiah, that's a mighty fine dog ya got there. Ain't much to look at, but he's something else out in those woods."

Samson came up to Jeremiah, sat down on its haunches, and looked up at its master, waiting to be petted. Its tail thumped against the ground. Jeremiah glanced at him, then scratched behind the dog's velvety ears. The misfit dog with a misfit master, living with two other misfits. But somehow they all seemed to fit together. At least Jeremiah thought so.

He knew Callie would take some convincing to believe it. A lot of convincing. He just hoped he was up to the task, for all their sakes.

They ate their squirrel stew in silence. Eli had assured them that the men were nowhere near their camp, and that building a fire would be safe. Eli wolfed down his food, but Jeremiah and Callie merely picked at the meal. The afternoon sunlight filtered through the swaying branches of the trees. Callie rose from her seat and retrieved their dishes. She let Samson have the leftovers.

"I'm going to bed," she announced, her voice barely audible.

"This early?" Eli asked. He leaned back against a large rock. "Ain't you feelin' well, gal?"

"I'm fine, just a little tired. I need to rest." She glanced at Jeremiah for the briefest of moments. "It's been a long day."

Jeremiah studied her, watching the shadows

of the leaves dance across her solemn face. Indeed she looked tired, both physically and emotionally. The dark crescents beneath her eyes and the sorrow in her expression said as much.

He stood, adjusting his sling as he rose. "Take my bed. I'll sleep out here tonight too."

She looked at him with dull eyes. "You don't have to."

"I want to. It's going to be a beautiful night. I'm sure Eli could use the company."

"Hmph." Eli crossed his legs at the ankles and picked at his teeth.

Jeremiah's gaze locked with Callie's for a moment. He willed her to understand that he only wanted her to be comfortable. She deserved to get not only a decent nap, but a good night's sleep too. That, along with much, much more.

"Okay." She turned around and went to the cart, shutting the doors behind her.

He stared at the back of the cart for a few moments, then sat back down.

"You smoke?"

Jeremiah looked at Eli. "No."

"Good, cause I ain't got nothin' for ya to smoke."

Jeremiah stared at the fire. The orange flames danced, thin spirals of black smoke wafting from their tips. It was mesmerizing, watching the heat's beautiful destruction. But it didn't take his thoughts off of Callie.

He turned to Eli, who had tipped his hat lower on his head and folded his arms across his chest. He looked ready to fall asleep, seemingly unaware of the turmoil around him. Jeremiah's gaze went back to the fire.

"She showed ya, didn't she?"

Jeremiah's head jerked in Eli's direction. "How did you know?"

"I could tell." He didn't look at Jeremiah, his gaze remaining fixed on the flickering heat in front of him.

"I don't understand it. How could her mother do that to her?"

"Boy, her mother was nothin' like Callie. She was cold. Calculatin'. Carin' only 'bout herself an' appearances. If Penelope Winters had been the one to find you on that road, she'd of run right over yer body an' not think twice 'bout it. That's the gospel truth."

"But her father—"

"Weak, weak man. Did everythin' the wife tole him to." Eli peered at Jeremiah from beneath his hat brim. "Women."

"Callie's different."

"Yer dang tootin' she's different. She's goodness through an' through." He looked back at the fire again. "That's why I hate what happened to her. What she's gotta live with ever' day. An' she's stuck with me on top of that."

"She loves you."

"I reckon so. I ain't done nothin' to deserve it, though." Eli lifted up his hat. "I also reckon she cares for you too. That's why she showed them scars to ya."

Jeremiah didn't answer for a long time. "I know," he finally admitted.

Eli brushed the dirt from his already dust-coated clothes. Then he gave Jeremiah a piercing glare. "Callie's been hurt afore. She feels unloveable, ya know. Ugly."

"She's *not* ugly."

"Of course she ain't," Eli said. "But she ain't had no one tell her any different, or show her any different. Me tellin' her she's purty don't count." He yawned, tipping his hat back over his eyes. "I could catch some winks too. Glad we had this little talk. Just one more thing—if ya hurt my Callie, I'm gonna have to kill ya." Settling back against the rock, he shut his eyes, ending the conversation.

Jeremiah, paused, a little surprised by the casual delivery of the threat, yet knowing Eli would see it through if he had to. Scrubbing a hand over his face, he thought about everything that had happened within the past few hours. Her gentle, but deft, touch as she cut his hair. The heartbreak in her eyes as she'd revealed her past.

All of a sudden an idea came to him, a way that he could make Callie see just how lovely she really was. And he knew just how to do it.

Chapter Fifteen

Callie woke up a few hours later with the usual pain in her back and shoulders. What was different was that she had her sleeping spot back. Jeremiah had insisted on it. It seemed chivalrous of him, but Callie knew the real reason why.

He felt sorry for her.

She rolled over and shut her eyes, trying to forget the embarrassment. The humiliation. The look of horror in his eyes when she'd showed him her scars. The pitiful expression on his face when she told him her story.

However, she couldn't avoid Jeremiah forever. Excusing herself for a nap had been a way of escape, but she couldn't keep hiding away.

Besides, even though she'd never have him, she still had her dignity and her pride. She would just continue on as if nothing had happened, as if he hadn't seen her ugliness. Pretending that things were completely normal should be simple enough to do.

If only she hadn't grown to care for him so much.

She had looked beneath his bruised body and angry outbursts and saw the real man deep inside. The one who had the courage to try to make something of himself apart from his family. The one who cared for a half-blind, mangy mutt that no one else could possibly want. The one who had tried to make her feel at ease, even when he was in pain himself.

How could she not care for him? And how could she ever let him go?

But she had to. He wouldn't stay with them much longer, not once he got his strength back. Once they reached the next town he would leave them behind. She would remain with Eli and whatever new schemes he would dream up. While she loved Eli in spite of his misguided intentions, she could barely think about going back to the life she'd lived before Jeremiah had come into their lives. Yet what other choice did she have?

Sitting up, she grabbed her hairbrush and began combing out the tangles in her hair. She yanked the bristles through the strands, sharp pinches of pain pricking her scalp. She barely noticed, not when it felt like daggers were impaling her heart and soul.

Quickly she blinked back her tears, swallowed the hard stone in her throat, and braided her hair. She inhaled a deep breath. She may have been wallowing in self-pity in private, but she would never let anyone else see that part of herself. She hadn't before and she wasn't about to start now. Especially not in front of Jeremiah.

Opening the door, she steeled herself, expecting to see him sitting near the fire, waiting for her to fix breakfast. From the position of the sun she could see she'd overslept. Hurriedly she scrambled out of the cart and walked to the fire pit.

There was no one in sight.

Puzzled, she scanned the landscape. A low fire burned in the pit, but there was nobody else around. Not even Samson. Shrugging, she went on and started making biscuits to go with supper, assuming the men would return shortly.

But long after the biscuits were shaped and ready to put over the fire, neither man nor dog had returned. Callie walked to the outer edge of their camp. "Eli? Jeremiah?" she called out. "Samson?"

No response.

Dread and worry pooled in her belly. Where could they have gone? She wasn't too concerned for Eli; he could take care of himself. But where was Jeremiah? He was too weak to be off in the woods for a lengthy period of time. Several scenarios ran through her mind, none of them good. What if he had passed out somewhere from weakness? Or what if he was hurt and couldn't get back to camp? What if he was lost?

Brushing the flour off her fingers, she picked up a lantern and some matches. The sun was dipping below the horizon and it would be dark soon. Praying she was heading in the right direction, she left the clearing and entered into the woods, heading for the stream and calling out Jeremiah's name.

As she plunged into the woods, the trees became thicker and were situated closer together. The daylight around her dimmed to gray. She called for him again. "Jeremiah?"

"Over here."

Relief rushed through her like a waterfall spilling over a cliff. Swiftly she scurried toward his voice, which was accompanied by the heightening sound of the rushing water. Emerging out of the trees, she saw him, reclining by the bank.

She couldn't help but smile a little. He made a rather odd picture, leaning back against his good arm, his bright blue and pink sling draped over a faded flannel shirt that seemed to swallow him. He was barefoot, and she noticed for the first time how short his pants were. His hair was tied back with a leather strap into a short curly tail at the back of his neck. Glancing over at her he smiled, but didn't get up. "Have a nice nap?"

His cavalier attitude toward her concern removed the smile from her face. "How could you worry me like that?"

"Why would you be worried?"

"Why?" She marched over to him. "Jeremiah, you're still not well. Something could have happened to you. You could have stumbled and fallen. Or fainted. Or—"

"Ah, so you *do* care." He sat up, wincing slightly.

"Well, of course I . . . care." She faltered as

his gaze connected with hers, his dark brown eyes mesmerizing. Silently he held out his hand to her. She clasped it, expecting to help him rise. Instead he pulled her down beside him with more strength than she could have imagined he possessed considering his injuries.

"Sit with me," he said, moving close beside her. "The sun is about to set."

"I've seen a sunset before." Instinctively she moved away from him.

"Well I haven't—not with you, anyway." He raised one knee and let his free arm dangle across it. "It's nice out here," he remarked, looking around. "I've been in California for more than a year and I never realized what pretty country it is."

"It does have its merits," she admitted.

"I've also come to realize something else. I don't appreciate things like I should. I never have." He looked at her. "Take my family, for instance. Back in Texas I had a fine home, a mother who loved me, and a brother with a new family I didn't even try to get to know. Instead I just packed up and left."

"You wanted a better future for yourself."

"No, I didn't. I wanted to hurt them. I wanted to go back someday, richer than Luke could ever hope to be, and show him that I could do fine without them. That I could be more successful than they'd ever thought I could be, and I would do it on my own. I wanted them to know I didn't need them."

Without thinking Callie touched his arm. "Everyone needs family, Jeremiah."

"I know that now. Too bad it took a year of poverty and a good beating for me to figure it out. That along with being around your family."

"Some family," she remarked bitterly.

"Hey, you have a great family. Don't let anyone tell you any different. You love and look out for each other. You care what happens to Eli and he cares what happens to you. But most importantly, you two accept each other for who you are, no questions asked. That is what real family is all about. I'll never be able to thank you enough for allowing me to be a part of it the past couple days."

"You don't have to thank me," she said softly. "You never have to thank me for anything. I helped you because I—"

"Care. I know that, Callie." He dropped his knee and squared his body, facing her directly.

He took her hand, holding tightly to it before she tried to snatch it away. He entwined his fingers in hers as if for good measure. His hand was strong and secure and felt more than wonderful. When he lightly squeezed her fingers her heartbeat doubled.

"I shore am tired, boss," Bart griped.

"Shut up." But Clark's remark didn't hold its usual sting. They had been traveling for two days with little water and almost no food. Bart wasn't the only one who was tired. Clark was beginning to give up hope that they would ever find the old man—and their gold.

Clark suddenly brought his horse to a halt. Bart nearly slammed into the back of them.

"What'd ya do that fer, boss?"

"Shh!" Clark raised his hand to silence him. "Do you hear that?"

Bart strained to listen. "Hear what?"

"Voices."

The men paused for a few moments. Bart slowly grinned. "I shore do, boss. I hear 'em alright."

Clark brought his finger to his lips, then slipped off his horse. Quietly, he tied the mare to the nearest tree, then gestured for Bart to do the same. For the first time his hapless partner did as requested. Stealthily they both sneaked through the woods.

Anticipation threaded through Clark. They were so close he could practically smell the gold. At least he would have if gold had a smell. It didn't matter. What mattered was that he was mere feet from victory.

And woe to the folks who stood between him and his treasure.

"I've been waiting to do this all day," he said, smiling.

"To hold my hand?"

"Yes. To touch you."

"Jeremiah—"

"Shhh. Don't say anything. Just listen. Listen and believe what I'm telling you, because it's the truth. You're beautiful, Calliope Winters. Both inside and out."

Her eyes widened. "But the scars—"

"What scars?" He grinned, running his thumb along her hand.

"That's not funny."

His smile faded. "It's not meant to be."

"Jeremiah, you don't know what you're saying. You haven't seen them . . . up close."

"Doesn't matter."

For the briefest of instants a surge of joy welled inside her, only to be quashed by harsh reality. He was still weak from the beating, still feeling indebted to her, possibly still feeling pity for her. "You don't know what you're saying," she said, extracting her hands from his.

He frowned. "Oh, so you think I'm crazy now. That my attackers clocked me on the head so hard that I can't see what's directly in front of me." Annoyance edged his tone.

"That's not what I meant and you know it."

"Awww, looky what we have here, boss."

Callie's head jerked up at the unfamiliar voice. She felt Jeremiah's arm quickly slide around her in a protective vise as two men on horseback came into the clearing.

"Seems we interrupted a little lover's spat here," the one in the black hat said. He had a black bandanna tied around his neck. His companion was short, his back even more hunched than Callie's. His leering gaze made her stomach turn.

Jeremiah suddenly stiffened against her. "You," he said in a venomous tone.

"Hey boss, he ain't dead after all!" The short man said.

"I can see that, Bart." He jumped down from his horse and pulled a gun out of his holster, pointing it directly at Jeremiah. "You cheated death once, greenhorn. I aim to make sure you don't cheat it again."

Chapter Sixteen

"Good biscuits," Bart said over a mouth full of food. White crumbs tumbled into his patchy beard. He picked up a tin cup and took a big gulp. "Coffee's good too. You should try some, boss."

"In a minute." The man in the black hat yanked on the knotted rope. "You two aren't going anywhere."

Frantically, Cassie dug her heels in the dirt and tried to free her hands, which were bound with Jeremiah's. The men had escorted them at gunpoint back to the camp and had tied them up. Jeremiah and Callie's backs were against each other, a large rope then wrapped around their bodies twice, also secured with a tight

151

knot. Fumbling with the rope on her wrist, she finally gave up.

Her breathing started to constrict with panic, but she tamped the emotion down. Falling apart wouldn't help their situation any. She had to remain calm.

Jeremiah hadn't moved. He hadn't made a sound either. He had to be in excruciating pain with his broken arm twisted that way. But he remained stony silent.

"So we meet again, greenhorn."

Jeremiah didn't respond.

The man walked over to the fire and sat down by Bart, then rested his gun on his knee, the barrel pointing straight at them. Their grungy faces glowed in the light of the flames. He grabbed a biscuit from Bart's hand and chewed on it. "What, cat got your tongue? Or maybe it was that mangy mutt of yours. Funny, don't see him around here, do you Bart?"

"Nope. But if I eva do, I'm gonna kill that thang. Plumb tore a hole in my britches the last time."

"How do you know these people?" Callie asked, her curiosity overriding her common sense.

"Tell her, greenhorn." The man's eyes gleamed darkly in the firelight. "Tell her how you know us." When Jeremiah didn't answer, the man spoke again, his black glare staring straight through Callie. "Guess he's not interested in answering your question, is he?"

Callie's blood ran cold. These men didn't seem very bright, but they had a loaded weapon and apparently little, if any, conscience. Stupidity and bullets were a deadly combination.

Another surge of panic struck her, this time right in her belly. *Where was Eli? He should have been back by now, with Samson. Where had he gone off to?*

"Here ya go, boss." Bart handed the man his coffee.

He grabbed it out of Bart's hand and took a gulp, then set it down on the ground. Taking his gun, he scratched beneath his chin with the point of the barrel. "Now, what do you suppose we should do with you two?

"Let her go," Jeremiah said through clenched teeth. "You can do anything you want with me, just let her go."

"I don't know 'bout that, greenhorn. She ain't

much to look at, but I bet we could still have a good time with her. Dontcha think so, Bart?"

"Oh yeah, boss." Bart let out a goofy giggle. "I can have lotsa fun with her."

"You lay a hand on her, I'll kill you!" Jeremiah lunged toward them with his shoulders, but the binds held tight.

The man scoffed. "Seein' as I'm the one holdin' the only gun 'round here, I believe I can do whatever I want." He rose from the stool and walked over to them. Standing in front of Callie, he ran one dirty, smelly hand down her cheek. She recoiled in disgust.

"Hey, she kinda looks like you, Bart, all hunched over like this." He took his gun and outlined her chin with the tip. "But it ain't her face we're interested in, now, is it."

"Nope," Bart piped up gleefully.

"Leave me alone!" Callie said. But her protest sounded weak and useless.

He laughed. "Or you're gonna do what? Have yer beau here save you?" He looked over at Jeremiah and smirked. "He'll be dead in a little while anyway."

"No!"

"Yes." He removed the gun and went back to the fire. "But not until I've had somethin' to eat.

I'll need my strength . . ." He gave Callie a lecherous look. ". . . for later."

Jeremiah bit on his bottom lip until he drew blood. Frustration and anger battled within him as he tried to loosen his binds. But without the full strength of his hands he couldn't do anything. He was helpless, as helpless as he'd been at the hands of these two dimwits the first time.

They were obviously a few cards minus a full deck, but they were also mean. And evil. Jeremiah had no doubt they would follow through on their threat to kill him. He couldn't bear to think what they would do to Callie. Despite the burning pain in his broken arm, he worked the rope again.

"It's no use," Callie whispered, her voice trembling. "I can't get mine undone either. Where's Eli?"

"Shh," Jeremiah hushed her. "I don't think they know he's around. If they had they would have said something. So don't say a word about him, okay?"

"O-okay."

He wasn't worried about Eli. The old man had decided to go hunting with Samson earlier in the day. Jeremiah silently prayed he would show up soon, although he had to admit he didn't know how a short old man with a crooked slingshot could take on these two criminals. Still, if Eli was anything he was resourceful.

The focus of his concern at the moment was Callie. Her body shook against his, and her fear tore at him. He didn't care what happened to him, but he wouldn't let them harm her. He had to do something instead of just sitting here, vulnerable. A thought suddenly struck him. "Hey, boss," he called out.

"Hey, he ain't your boss," Bart piped up. "He's mine. You call him Clark like ever'one else does."

"Bart!" Clark snapped, glaring at his partner for giving out his true name. Then he let out a long-suffering sigh and turned back to Jeremiah. "What do ya want?"

"I take it you didn't find my claim."

Clark's eyebrow shot up. "What makes ya think that?"

"If you had found my claim, you wouldn't be here."

"Maybe we ain't interested in yer claim," Clark retorted.

"Yes, we is, boss," Bart said. "We searched high low for it, don't you 'member? Then we went to that minin' camp and started playin' cards an'—"

Clark reached out and smacked Bart upside the head. "As I was sayin', we ain't interested in yer claim." He looked at Jeremiah, then tore off a piece of biscuit and shoved it in his mouth. "Ain't you got anythin' else to eat 'round here?"

"No," Callie squeaked.

"I'll make you a deal," Jeremiah interjected. "You let her go, and I'll take you to my claim."

"An' what makes you think I'd be stupid 'nuff to believe you?"

"Think about it. You're the one with the gun. I have a broken arm. It's two against one. How can I be a threat to you?"

Tilting his head to the side, Clark appeared to be mulling over Jeremiah's words. "What if yer lyin'? Yer claim's far from here, how would you be able to find it?"

"We're near Sacramento, right?"

Clark nodded.

"Then I know exactly where my claim is." Jeremiah looked directly at him. "You think I'd forget where I found my gold? In fact, we were just heading back there."

"You was?" Bart piped up.

Jeremiah could see he had the two

scoundrels' rapt attention. They wouldn't need much more convincing. "We were heading out in the morning. But if you let her go, we could leave tonight. We'd be back at the claim in two days, tops."

Clark stroked his stubbly chin, as if in deep thought. "What if we just took both of ya with us?"

"Then you'll never find the gold."

Lifting his gun, he pointed it at Jeremiah. "Oh, we'll find that gold alright. I think we can make you tell us."

Callie's heart stopped beating at the sight of the gun aimed at Jeremiah's chest. *What was he doing? Why was he baiting these men? Couldn't he see they were eager for a chance to kill him?* "Jeremiah," she hissed in a choked whisper.

"Shh. I know what I'm doing, Callie."

"Quit yer whisperin' over thar." Clark stood up, still keeping the Colt trained on Jeremiah. "I'm callin' the shots here, not you, greenhorn. Yer gonna tell me whar that claim is, or else."

"Or else what? You'll shoot me? Go ahead."

"No!" Callie cried. "Jeremiah, what are you doing?"

"Go on and shoot," he continued, ignoring her. "But if I'm dead, you'll never find the gold."

Clark turned and pointed the gun at Callie. Her heart leapt to her throat.

"I reckon she can tell us," he said. "Seein' as you two are so close, I'm sure you told her whar the claim was."

She pulled back. "No, no, he didn't tell me anything!"

"Don't believe her, boss," Bart said, shuffling up beside him. "She's lyin'."

"She doesn't know anything about the claim or about the gold," Jeremiah said.

"Please," she begged, truly terrified now. "Don't hurt me."

"Let her go." Jeremiah's tone was low and menacing. "Right now. Then you'll have your gold. That's the deal. She walks away from here alive, and you become a rich man."

Keeping the gun steady on Callie, Clark looked from Jeremiah to her, then back to Jeremiah again. Finally he lifted the Colt. "Untie her, Bart."

"But boss—"

"I said untie her! We don't need her anyway."

Bart's lip lowered in a pout. "But I was wantin' a piece of her."

"We'll be able to buy better women once we get that gold. Now move it along."

Before she could think straight, Bart had unbound the knots, freeing her. As soon as her wrists slipped through the rope, he grabbed Jeremiah by the shirt and hoisted him up. His hands were still tied behind his back.

Clark walked over to Jeremiah and pointed the gun at his head. "Hitch up them mules, Bart. We'll take them and that old tinker's cart with us. You," he said, tipping his head toward Callie. "Run along now. The rest of us have some travelin' to do."

"No," she cried, moving toward Jeremiah. She'd gone three steps when she heard the click of the gunhammer being pulled back.

"You don't wanna do that," he said. "Yer loverboy here's givin' you a second chance. I'd take it if I were you."

"But Jeremiah—"

"He's comin' with us. So ya might as well say yer good-bye's now, 'cause ya ain't ever seein' him again."

Clark's words ran through her like a sharp blade.

"Go," Jeremiah said, his voice hoarse. He swallowed convulsively.

"I-I can't." Her eyes were locked with his. She could see something inside them, an emotion she felt deep inside her soul, one that quelled her fear. She knew once the men found the claim they would kill him. He knew that too. He was sacrificing himself to keep her alive. Tears sprang to her eyes. Couldn't he see how pointless that was? She didn't want to live without him.

"No," she said, crossing her arms. "I'm not leaving."

"Callie—" Jeremiah pleaded.

"What are ya, a bloomin' idiot?" Clark said. "Go on, get outta here. Yer standin' in the way of my gold."

"Then I guess you aren't getting your gold, because I'm not leaving Jeremiah behind."

"Oh, for the love of—" Clark uncocked the Colt and shoved Jeremiah to the ground. Callie ran over and knelt beside him.

Jeremiah looked up at her, anger sparking in his eyes. "What are you doing?"

"I told you, I'm not going."

"Callie, please." The fury distilled into a solemn plea. "I couldn't take it if anything happened to you."

She cupped his cheek, caressing his jawline

with her thumb. "Whatever happens, we'll face it together."

To her surprise he smiled, then nodded. Wincing as he tried to get into a sitting position, she reached an arm around him and helped him sit up, then cast the men a defiant glare.

Clark sneered. He aimed the gun at them. "I've had enough of these two. Gold or no gold, its time fer them to meet their maker."

Chapter Seventeen

"No one's meetin' their maker today. 'Cept maybe you two fellas."

Clark turned around at the sound of the raspy voice. Jeremiah breathed a small sigh of relief. Eli! Samson was right beside him, baring his sharp teeth.

"Now, you jest step away from my Callie and her man nice an' slow, ya hear?" Eli held a sawed-off shotgun level to Clark's chest. He flicked a gaze over to Bart. "That means you too."

Samson growled and lunged at Bart.

Bart held up his hands and backed away. "Okay, okay, I'll do anythin'. Jest git that mutt away from me!"

"Samson!" Jeremiah called.

After sending out one last low growl, Samson trotted over to Jeremiah and Callie, then sat right next to them as if standing guard.

"Drop yer gun," Eli ordered Clark as he moved toward him. "Drop it or I'll blast yer worthless head into a million bits an' pieces."

Slowly, Clark laid down his gun next to Jeremiah's feet.

"Untie me, Callie," Jeremiah said.

Instantly she did as he asked. He picked up the gun and held it in one hand then aimed it at Clark. His broken arm hung limply by his side.

"Here." Eli went over and took the bandanna off of Clark. "Use this. He ain't got no need of it now. Besides, these here two owe me a pair of pants."

Jeremiah cast Eli an odd look as the old man quickly wrapped his arm in a haphazard sling. "Your pants?"

"Long story." Eli tossed the shotgun carelessly on the ground.

Jeremiah, Clark, and Bart all jumped. "What'd you do that for?" Bart hollered. "That dadgum thing could have gone off!"

Eli grinned. "Nah. Trigger's rusty. Ain't been able to fire a shot in years."

*   *   *

An hour later, Clark and Bart were securely fastened to a nearby tree. The thieves weren't going anywhere. Jeremiah and Eli decided that the next day they would head for Sacramento and turn them into the authorities.

Although Callie and Jeremiah were seated next to each other around the campfire, there was ample space between them. He had seemed completely engrossed in helping Eli tie up the men, and he was just as absorbed in hearing Eli relay how he had come upon them in the clearing.

"I heard the whole thing, while I was hidin' up in that tree thar." Eli poured a cup of coffee as he continued his tale.

"You were up in the tree?" Callie asked, his admission capturing her attention. "Eli, remember what happened the last time you climbed a tree."

"Yeah, but I'm sober now." He sat up a little straighter. "I've been sober for a while, haven't I? Well whaddaya know 'bout that? Anyhoo, I shimmied up the tree—Samson had the good sense to stay quiet—and I listened to it all. These are the rascals I won the gold off of."

"Ya stole our gold, ya buzzard!" Bart hollered.

"Shut yer yap!" Eli retorted, then looked to Jeremiah again. "As I was sayin' I got the gold from them—"

"Wait." Jeremiah leaned forward. "You got your gold from them?"

"Uh-huh."

"How much?" His voice raised with excitmement.

"A lot. They was in these two leather pouches—"

"Can I see them?"

Callie had never seen him so animated. "Jeremiah, what is it?" she asked, as Eli rose to retrieve the bags.

"Callie, these men were the ones who beat me up. I was leaving my claim, heading for Sacramento, carrying my gold. Clark was right about one thing, I am a greenhorn, because I was stupid enough to carry them in plain sight. They jumped me, took the gold . . . well, you know the rest."

The pieces finally fell into place. "It's your gold," Callie said slowly. "That's how they knew about your claim. We've had your gold the whole time and didn't know it."

"Seems that way." Jeremiah turned around to see what was taking Eli so long. "But there's only one way to know for sure. The pouches were stamped with my initials."

Callie leapt up as Eli returned to the fireside. Jeremiah followed her.

"Here ya go." Eli tossed him a pouch. Jeremiah caught it with his one good hand. "The other one's the same as this."

Jeremiah turned it over in his hand, bending down and holding the leather bag near the fire. He gripped it as the letters "JJ" were illumined by the flames.

"It's mine," he whispered, scarcely believing his eyes. "My gold."

Callie sat back down. She watched as he fumbled with the pouch and opened it, pouring a few of the nuggets on the ground. His eyes widened as he picked one up and examined it eagerly. He had regained all he had lost—his gold and soon his health.

A painful wave of understanding crashed into Callie. Jeremiah had regained what he'd lost. He didn't need her anymore.

She fought the disappointment plummeting through her, silently berating herself for her selfish thoughts. She loved him, she knew that now. She should be happy for him, not upset. Tamping down her emotions, she rose and walked over to Eli. "Go get the rest of it," she told in a tone that brooked no argument.

Eli looked at her as if to quarrel, then his countenance fell. "Fine." He slogged his way back to the cart, mumbling bitterly all the way. He returned shortly, still clutching it in his hand. "Don't suppose we can keep jest a little as a reeward?"

She shook her head. "It belongs to Jeremiah."

"Dadburn it." Eli dropped the bag in her outstretched hand. Scowling, he went to the opposite side of the fire and plopped down next to Samson.

Callie knelt next to Jeremiah and lightly touched his good arm. "Here's the other pouch."

He turned and accepted the gold, amazement still shining in his eyes. "I can't believe I got it back, Callie. I got it all back."

Despite her heart breaking inside, she managed to smile a little. "I'm happy for you, Jeremiah." Then, before he could see the tears aching in her eyes, she stood and walked away.

Jeremiah watched Callie head for the tinker's cart. He'd seen the sheen in her eyes as she had handed him his gold. She was clearly upset, and he had to find out why. He got up, shoved the gold into his pocket and followed her, meeting her just as she reached the other side of the cart. Her back was to him.

"Callie, what's wrong?" he asked, sensing she was about to shut him out again.

"Nothing," she replied, keeping her back to him and lighting a small lantern. She picked up Eli's ratty bedroll. Her voice sounded thick, but she kept right on talking. "Eli will have to stand watch over those two scoundrels tonight; I'm sure they'll try something. He'll need this, and probably a blanket. He shouldn't be too comfortable, though, or he might fall asleep. Of course, I'll have to fix some supper first, those men ate all our biscuits and I'm sure everyone's hungry—"

"Callie." Jeremiah's voice was stern. He didn't want to talk about Eli, or supper, and he certainly didn't want to keep talking to her back. He put his hand on her shoulder and gently turned her toward him. To his surprise, she didn't pull away. The tears that had shone in her eyes moments earlier now rolled freely down her cheeks. Something tugged deep inside him. Ignoring the pain in his broken arm, he wrapped her in his embrace.

"Shhh," he said, stroking her hair with his free hand. "It's okay, Callie. Everything's all right. They can't hurt you anymore." He remembered the fear in her eyes when the thieves had tied them up. He also remembered how brave she was . . . and how she wouldn't leave his side. His arm tightened around her.

"Jeremiah," she choked out, trying to wriggle free from him yet again.

This time he wouldn't let her go. No, he *couldn't* let her go. Not now, not ever.

She pressed her hands against his chest and looked up at him. "I can't do this."

He stared down at her tear-stained face. "Do what? Let me hold you? Let me get close to you?" He grinned. "Well, too bad darlin' because that's all I'm wanting to do right now."

Her eyes grew wide with surprise. "It is?"

"Yep."

"But why?"

His smile faded. "How could you ask me that question, Callie? There are a million reasons why I want to be with you. You're sweet, and kind—"

She looked away, but he tilted her chin toward him. "And very, very beautiful."

Her eyes closed briefly, then opened again.

He could see the doubt in them, and he knew there was only one way he could convince her. Leaning forward, his lips hovering over hers, he captured her mouth with his, his kiss telling her more than he could ever put into words.

"Now do you believe me?" he asked, hoping she was as affected by their kiss as he was.

"Yes," she replied, her cheeks adorably red and her voice breathless.

The combination was irresistible. He kissed her again, slowly and thoroughly. When they finally parted, she stared up at him.

"I was so afraid you were going to leave," she said.

"Oh, Callie, you couldn't get rid of me if you tried." He kissed her forehead and drew her against him.

"Calliope!"

They both turned at the sound of Eli's cranky voice. He appeared from the other side of the cart, his expression harsh. "When we gonna have some vittles? I'm starvin' . . ." His voice trailed away and his craggy face softened at the sight of Callie and Jeremiah still locked in each other's arms. "Well, I'll be," he said softly. Then he cleared his throat. "Guess me and Samson can round up something." Without another word he spun around and left. Jeremiah heard him whistle for the dog.

He glanced down at Callie, the low light of the lantern casting a warm glow on her face. Happiness shown in her eyes and played on the smile on her lips. He couldn't help but kiss her one more time, deeply satisfied when he heard her sigh and lean against him.

Jeremiah's heartbeat thumped against Callie's cheek. It all seemed surreal, the two of them standing here with his good arm tightly around her, the tingle of his kiss still flowing through her. Lifting her head, she looked up at him. "What do we do now?"

His hand came up and cupped her cheek. She could feel the scratches and calluses on his skin, the roughness caused by months and months of digging for his elusive fortune. Now he had it, and a brand new future. She so desperately wanted to be a part of it.

"The first thing we need to do is head for Sacramento and turn Clark and Bart over to the authorities. Then . . ." A twinkle appeared in his eye.

"Then what?" She eyed him skeptically. "Jeremiah Jackson, what are you up to?"

"I figure we could find a preacher in a town that size, don't you?"

"A preacher? What do we need . . ." Happiness welled inside her as she realized what he meant. "Oh, Jeremiah," she said, throwing her arms around his neck and squeezing him tight. Then just as quickly, niggling doubt assaulted her. She stepped away from him. "Are you sure?"

He nodded, causing an errant lock of curly hair to fall across his forehead. "Honey, I've never been more sure of anything in my life. I love you, Callie, and I want you to be my wife. If you'll have me, that is."

"If I'll have you?" Callie burst into laughter, and then with boldness she hadn't known she possessed, reached her hand behind his head and pulled him down for a soul-stirring kiss.

"So I take it you'll marry me?" Jeremiah quipped as they pulled apart.

"Of course, I'll marry you. I love you, Jeremiah." She stepped into his open embrace. "I love you so very much.

Later that evening, after a supper of roasted rabbit and biscuits, Jeremiah, Callie, and Eli sat around the fire. Clark and Bart, still tied to the tree, had both fallen asleep, their stubbly chins bobbing against their sweat-stained shirts. Eli had retrieved their horses and they were tied up to a couple of trees on the perimeter of the campsite.

Callie and Jeremiah sat next to each other, her arm linked in his, her head on his shoulder. Fatigue permeated every bone in her body, but peace filtered throughout her mind and soul. She and Jeremiah were together, and would be for the rest of their lives.

Several minutes later, Jeremiah shifted on his stool. Callie's head bobbed up as he reached inside his pants pocket and pulled one of the pouches of gold out of his pocket. Wordlessly he handed it to Eli, who was seated across from them.

"I reckon I don't know what to say," Eli said gruffly. He stared down at the money in his hand. " 'Cept thank you."

Jeremiah smiled. "That's enough."

Callie, still in disbelief, couldn't grasp that they would never have to worry about finances again. "We've never had this much money before," she said. "What will we do with all of it?"

"Gal, we'll find plenty to do with it," Eli said. "An' I promise ya, yer gonna have a real home."

He touched her arm lightly. "Just like you always wanted."

Jeremiah grasped her hand, holding it tight. He kissed her temple. "I know exactly where we'll find one."

Chapter Eighteen

August, 1852

"I don't know if I can do this."

Callie hooked her arm around her husband's bent elbow. "Yes, you can, Jeremiah. We've come this far. There's no turning back now."

Jeremiah gripped the reins in his hand. He almost had full use of his arm now. As he and Callie sat in the buckseat of their brand new covered wagon, he scanned the seemingly endless pasture land. The Texas summer beat down on them, causing rivulets of perspiration to flow down his back. He glanced at Callie, decked out in a light yellow dress with little pink flowers all over it—one of about a dozen they'd purchased in Sacramento. Tiny pearl earrings gleamed in her earlobes.

He tugged at the collar of his chambray shirt. "What if . . . what if he turns me away?"

"Your brother wouldn't do that. If he's half the man you are, he'll welcome you with open arms."

Jeremiah leaned over and kissed her lightly on the corner of her mouth. "I appreciate the vote of confidence."

"Good. So now that you're all confident—"

"Who said I was confident?" He looked down at the reins, loosening his grip on them. Deep indentations from the leather appeared on his palm. "I'm a nervous wreck."

"You shouldn't be. They're family. I'm sure they've missed you as much as you missed them."

"Maybe. But what I did to them was stupid."

"And selfish and unforgivable." She removed her arm from his. "We've been over this all before. How long are you going to use your past as an excuse to escape the future?"

He sighed. "You're right. Of course."

"Of course I am. Now lets head for the house." Callie flipped open a large, lacy fan. "I'm melting away in this heat."

"Why, Mrs. Jackson, I do believe you're becoming quite the lady," Jeremiah teased, slapping the reins against the horse's flanks.

"Why, Mr. Jackson, I guess I am."

They rode along the straight dirt trail for several moments. Then suddenly Callie reached out and grabbed Jeremiah's arm. He halted the horses again and turned to her.

"Callie, honey, what's wrong?"

"What if they don't like me?" she asked, her voice small and quiet, much like it had been when they first met.

"Now look who's being ridiculous—"

"I'm being serious. We haven't been married that long, only a couple months. What if your family doesn't think I'm good enough for you?"

"Oh, Callie," he said, enfolding her in his arms. She had made great strides since that day months ago when she'd shown him her scars. But there were moments, like this one, when her insecurities overwhelmed her. "Honey, they'll adore you. How can they not?" He stroked her hair, then held her from him. "And if they don't, then we'll leave. It's not as if we can't afford to live anywhere we want to. With the money we've got from selling the claim to the mining company, and that reward for capturing Clark and Bart, we can move to England if you want to."

She shook her head. "I don't want that. I want to be here with you, where you want to be." Her hand swept out, gesturing to the land surrounding them. "This is where your home is."

"And it will be our home." He kissed the tip of her nose. "Let's go."

Luke Jackson lifted up the last pitchfork full of hay and tossed it into the stall. The temperature was sweltering inside the barn, but mucking the stables was overdue. Normally he had the boys take care of it, but they were out helping his mother and Melanie weed the garden. Wiping the sweat from his brow on the back of his bare forearm, he entered the stall and began spreading out the hay.

"Thought you might like this."

He leaned back and peeked around the stall's opening. Melanie was standing in the barn doorway, a small bucket with a dipper in her hand. Grinning, he dropped the pitchfork and went to her.

After drinking a few dipperfuls of the clear, cold water, he kissed her cheek. "Thanks. I really needed that."

She frowned, her cute, heart-shaped mouth puckering into a pout. "That's it?"

"What?"

"That's *all* I get for carrying this big, heavy bucket all that long way from the pump house?"

"The pump house is no more than ten steps from here." He moved closer to her. "And that bucket hardly weighs a thing. But if you think I've been neglectful in showing my appreciation, then let me rectify that right now."

Melanie giggled as he swept her in his arms. Drawing her close, he nibbled on her neck. She shrieked with laughter as he tickled the side of her waist.

The sound of someone clearing his throat broke them apart.

Luke stared at the two figures in the doorway. Releasing his arm from Melanie's waist, he rubbed his eyes, unable to believe what he was seeing.

"Hi, Luke," Jeremiah said softly, holding his hat in his hand. His fingers worried the brim.

"Jeremiah?" Luke strode forward, quickly closing the distance between them. Without another word he yanked his brother into a fierce hug.

Unbidden, tears rolled down Jeremiah's face

as he held onto his brother. It was as if two years of heavy burdens had melted away. He was home. Here in San Antonio, at Jackson Ranch. And he didn't ever want to leave it again.

Luke pulled away from him, wiping his eyes with the heel of his hand. "I didn't think we'd ever see you again," he said in a thick voice.

Jeremiah stepped away from Luke and looked at Melanie. "I'm sorry for how I treated you when you first came here. You, the kids, Luke . . . all of you. And I'm sorry for taking off like that. I guess I left you here in a lurch, Luke."

"That doesn't matter," he said. "I'm the one who should be telling you I'm sorry. I did treat you like a little kid. After you left I finally realized everything you had done to keep this place running, and I had taken it for granted. I don't blame you for being angry with me. Can you forgive me?"

Jeremiah grinned. "There's nothing to forgive. It's all forgotten."

Melanie came toward him, her eyes wet with tears. She put her thin arms around his neck. "Welcome home, Jeremiah."

He returned her embrace with a tight one of his own, then moved away. "I didn't come alone. I brought someone with me."

"Who?" Luke asked.

Jeremiah reached behind the outside barn wall and took Callie's hand. "My wife," he said, leading her into the doorway. "Calliope Jackson, this is my brother, Luke, and his wife, Melanie."

"You're married?" Luke asked, sizing Callie up and down.

Callie gripped Jeremiah's hand tightly. He could tell Luke's appraisal put her on edge. He opened his mouth to say something when Luke stepped in front of her.

"I reckon she's a good, strong woman if she can put up with the likes of you, Jeremiah." He held out his arms to her. "Welcome to the family."

"Hey, watcha doin' leavin' me in that hot ol' wagon?" Eli and Samson trotted to Jeremiah and Callie. "Ya gone and left yer dog too." Eli scratched behind his ears. "Ain't no one givin' a hoot 'bout ya but me, boy."

Luke looked at Eli, then Jeremiah. "And this is?"

"My father-in-law," Jeremiah said. "Sort of."

"Eli Wallach, at yer service." He held out a brawny hand to Luke. "An' I'm guessin' ya already know Samson."

Samson barked in agreement.

"Seems we Jacksons have a habit of spring-ing surprises," Luke said, shaking Eli's hand. "But if you're a friend of Jeremiah's, then you're a friend of mine."

"We should find your mother," Melanie said, already standing at Callie's side. "She'll be so excited to see you. Callie, I can't wait to intro-duce you to my children. They'll be thrilled to have a new aunt. And our daughter, Rosalita, just started walking. It's the sweetest thing."

The women headed off toward the house, Eli and Samson close behind them. Jeremiah stayed back with Luke. He turned and looked at his brother. "It's a long story."

"Must be. I'm looking forward to hearing about it."

"So you forgive me?" Jeremiah asked, hold-ing his breath, unsure of what he'd do if Luke didn't.

Luke clapped him on the shoulder and led him out of the barn. "There's nothing to for-give. You're here, and that's all that matters."

Jeremiah grinned as they strode toward the house. *He's right. Being home is the only thing that matters.*

* * *

Jeremiah came up behind Callie and wrapped his arms around her, pulling her against his chest. She leaned into him as he rested his chin on her head.

"Eli still in there talking to your mother?"

"Yes, believe it or not. She hasn't left the table since he started waxing poetic about his escapades."

Callie giggled. "I think they're smitten with each other."

Jeremiah rolled his eyes. "Lord help us if they are."

They remained silent for a moment. "It's beautiful," she suddenly said, staring into the horizon.

He took in the soft, pastel-hued view from the porch of the ranch house. The colors cast the landscape in a warm glow of the lightest purples, pinks, oranges, and reds. "I dreamed about seeing this," he murmured, swaying her gently. "Of watching the sunset . . . with you."

"A San Antonio sunset," she said.

"Nothing better."

"Oh, yes, there is." She turned in his arms and tilted her face up to his. "I can think of about a hundred things better. And they all have to do with you."

He moved to kiss her, but she ducked out of his arms.

"You'll have to catch me first!" Laughing, she shuffled away.

Watching her as she ran, his love for her overwhelmed him. Her movements weren't fast, and it would only take a few strides before he would catch her. They both knew that. But that wasn't the point. She was smiling. Laughing. Happy. Just as he was happy, here at home, with the woman and family he loved.

With lumbering steps he chased after her, sweeping her up in his arms when he caught her behind the barn. Laying her down in the sweet smelling grass, he smoothed back the flyaway strands of hair from her forehead. Her smile faded as she brought her hand to his cheek. "I love you, Jeremiah Jackson."

"And I love you, Callie Jackson."

They kissed as the fading light of the sunset gave way to the sparkling new night.